The laught... ...ging Jane. She extended he... ...lunged for Ned Lynch.

Suddenly, she found the tip of Lynch's blade resting lightly on her bosom. It gave one twitch, slicing the cord that fastened her dress at the neck, and she felt a rush of air as the cloth fell partly away.

"Lesson Number One," Lynch said softly. "Do not get provoked."

Lynch flicked his sword upward from the sand, showering grit into her face and eyes.

"Lesson Number Two: forget fair play when you fight for your life."

She crashed to her knees and felt her sword wrenched from her hand—Ned Lynch had stepped on the blade and was standing over her.

"Lesson Number Three: never raise your sword to Ned Lynch unless you are prepared to die."

Universal®
An MCA Company
presents

A Jennings Lang—Elliott Kastner
Production

ROBERT SHAW
JAMES EARL JONES
PETER BOYLE
GENEVIEVE BUJOLD
BEAU BRIDGES
GEOFFREY HOLDER

in

SWASHBUCKLER

co-starring

Avery Schreiber
Anjelica Huston
Tom Clancy
Bernard Behrens
Dorothy Tristan

Executive Producer Elliott Kastner
Screenplay by Jeffrey Bloom
Story by Paul Wheeler
Produced by Jennings Lang
Directed by James Goldstone

Filmed in Panavision®
Color by Technicolor®

SWASHBUCKLER

D. R. Bensen

Based on the screenplay by Jeffrey Bloom
From a story by Paul Wheeler

SWASHBUCKLER
A Bantam Book / August 1976

ISBN 0-553-10245-1

Published simultaneously in the United States and Canada.

Bantam Books are published by Bantam Books, Inc. Its trademark, consisting of the words "Bantam Books" and the portrayal of a bantam, is registered in the United States Patent Office and in other countries. Marca Registrada. Bantam Books, Inc., 666 Fifth Avenue, New York, New York 10019.

PRINTED IN THE UNITED STATES OF AMERICA

Swashbuckler

Chapter 1

Nick Debrett's one eye took the scene in critically. It had a certain grim pageantry, if you cared for that sort of thing: the double file of red-coated soldiers, each bearing a musket, preceded by three drummers performing sharply rattling rolls on their instruments, and followed by the strutting major and the waddling chaplain, his rich purple face and corpulent figure a testimony to the opportunities for good food and drink afforded by a noncombatant commission in a British regiment on colonial duty.

The trouble was the setting, Debrett decided. Against the early-morning tropic sky, the bright green of the hills, and the softly pastel-hued houses of Kingston, Jamaica's greatest port, the redcoats looked out of place. They would have done very well to brighten a barracks square in foggy, damp England, or to show up clearly on a muddy European battlefield so that their generals could maneuver them like living chessmen—and their foes have a good target for their fire—but here they looked alien and ridiculous.

With parade-ground precision, the file of soldiers marched along the lower buttresses of the great, brooding fortress to a dock at the water's edge, and came to a halt with a final flourish of the drums. It was then that the air of military superefficiency broke down. It was clear that nobody—at least, not the major in command—had any idea of what to do next.

Major Folly. . . . Nick Debrett had thought it a

sardonic nickname devised by the troops, and very well suited to the pompously zealous young man who combined an evident sense of his rank and position, as well as the dashing figure he cut, with nearly total ignorance of how to command his men's respect. Then Nick had heard a sergeant address the major, and had realized that "Folly" was, in delicious actuality, the officer's family name.

The troops were evidently relishing the situation, though careful to preserve the wooden manner considered proper to their station. Debrett's sharp ears caught a muttered comment from the rear of the file: "Folly-Dolly's like to have himself hanged, 'stead o' the pris'ner, if he don't figure out what to do."

And it was true that the major—an excited and nervous corporal flanking him and the chaplain toiling in his wake—had mounted the thirteen steps that led to the wide gallows platform, and now seemed distinctly ill-at-ease as he glanced at the stark L-shaped gibbet. He was all too aware that, in his elaborate uniform, he presented the appearance of a gentleman highwayman about to swing on Tyburn Hill. There should, he knew, be a simple yet crisply military order that was prescribed for getting the condemned man and the two soldiers escorting him up the stairs, but what it was escaped him at the moment.

Major Folly, though fond of reading stirring accounts of warfare and the tactics of the great generals, had an imperfect grasp of the military vocabulary, and would feel almost sick when obliged to choose a command that would get a body of men from *here* to *there*, all facing the right way. He suspected that the men in his charge took a malicious delight in obeying him literally, no matter what the ensuing confusion. Folly knew that even a simple "Forward, march!" shouted at the prisoner's escort was fraught with danger—one of the escort was off to one side of the stairs, and would doubtless march right past them at the order.

Folly gritted his teeth and made an ambiguous but vigorous gesture, glaring savagely at the prisoner and the soldiers guarding him; with any luck, they would see what he meant and get themselves up on the platform.

The whole situation tickled Nick Debrett's sense of the absurd. He would have enjoyed it thoroughly—had he not been the man who was to hang from the gallows, neck stretched by the noose the soldier on his left was holding draped over one arm.

The soldier on his other side nudged him, and he moved forward to the steps and mounted them, made clumsy by the shackles around his ankles; his hands were chained in front of him, and he could not use his arms to help maintain balance. Major Folly moved back as Debrett approached, looking at him with a self-satisfied blandness that approached stupidity. Most men, Debrett knew, tended to be sensibly wary in his presence, but, from Folly's expression, the man passing in front of him might have been a starving, stunted chimney sweep instead of a giant, one-eyed black with the second most fearsome reputation in the Indies.

Best I start composing my last words, Nick Debrett thought. When a pirate was hanged in chains, it was the expected thing for him to come up with a speech of repentance and exhortation for the spectators not to follow in his bloody footsteps; at least, after each such execution, broadsheet peddlers sold quantities of "true-and-authentick" copies of such speeches. Debrett privately considered that the broadsheet printers made up the speeches themselves, and that most pirates' last words would, if printed, have been burned by the authorities.

However . . . His lips worked as he constructed a suitable farewell to the world. Ah, got it!

> The pirate who plunders the seas
> Lives a life that is foreign to ease.
> If he 'scape sword and shot,
> Then his end, like as not,
> Is dangling aloft in the breeze.

Ned Lynch would have liked that, if he'd been able to hear it, though there wasn't really enough bawdry in it for him. They'd had a lot of good times improvising verses in that strange meter Ned claimed was the native art of his home county of Limerick, in Ireland. Was there something he could do with Folly's name for a nice, derisive last effort? "And no more wits than poor Polly" would be an obvious finishing line, but working out the other "-olly" rhyme and the short third and fourth lines looked like taking more time than he had.

Debrett was suddenly convinced that his white eye patch was slipping, and his pinioned arms twitched with the instinctive beginning of the ordinary business of adjusting it; but the chains bit into his wrists. I'll never even do that again, he thought. Or anything.

The scrawny private on his left drove an elbow savagely into his side. "None o' that, blacky," he muttered. "You can skylark all you like at the rope's end, but keep it quiet till then."

"My eye patch—it's slipping," Debrett rumbled. "Forgot I couldn't reach it."

"A minute or so from now, that eye'll see as good's the other one," the soldier said spitefully. "Any road, you won't need no patches, slippin' or not. Here—why don't I take it off you now, a bit of a keepsake of Red Ned Lynch's lieutenant, Nick Debrett's fancy white-satin eye patch."

The man on Debrett's right turned and whispered harshly, "Bagot, next time you abuse a prisoner, count on it that you'll be emptying officers' chamber pots for the rest of your enlistment." He reached up and adjusted Debrett's patch. "There you are, all lined up again. Man may have to hang, but there's no reason he should look foolish whilst he's at it."

Folly, searching his memory of the manual of *The King's Regulations* he had read so assiduously yet vainly, now seemed to be clear on what the next step should be. "Corporal?"

The spit-and-polish noncom in front of him saluted smartly. "Sir?"

"The orders, Corporal."

"Sir!" He opened a leather pouch that hung from a

shoulder strap, took out a roll of paper secured with a stamped blob of red sealing wax, broke the seal, and handed it across to Major Folly.

The major handed it back. "No, Corporal," he said gently. *"You're* supposed to read it. I hold His Majesty's commission as a major of infantry, not as a town crier."

"Sir, yes, sir, no, sir," the flustered corporal said, retrieving the scroll. He opened it and brought it close to his eyes, which were squinting nervously. He was not used to reading at all, let alone aloud, and felt very foolish. How were you supposed to read an execution order, anyway? You couldn't bawl it out like a drill command, surely? It ought to sound impressive and official. Remembering the interminable Sunday sermons, he broke into an unctuous whine that brought the chaplain out of his somnolence with a startled glare of outrage.

" 'I, James Durant, in my capacity as acting governor and acting lord chief justice, do hereby decree that at dawn on the morrow' . . . we're a bit behindhand, sir," he said in a confidential aside to Folly.

"Never *mind,* Corporal! Just get to the gist of it, otherwise we'll be behind . . ." He seemed unable to complete the phrase elegantly, and stopped, not hearing the mutter of the soldier who had adjusted Debrett's patch: "How about behind-arse? That's the way he handles most things."

"Yes, sir," the corporal said. " '. . . that the malefactor Nicholas Debrett be placed in gibbet irons . . .' We had no gibbet irons on the island, sir, though," he pointed out.

Folly's fingers drummed on the hilt of the dress sword at his side. "That is apparent, Corporal. That the prisoner is festooned with odd bits of chain the armorer seemingly had no further use for is perhaps regrettable, but they will serve their function."

"I went so far as to ask at the ironmongers', sir, but they had no—"

"Continue, Corporal," Folly said, looking at him with dislike. "Continue."

Hurt at having his helpfulness—attempted helpfulness, anyhow—ignored, the corporal found his place in the order and went on, ". . . decree, yes, yes, malefactor . . . gibbet irons . . . oh, yes. 'The capital penalty will be paid. He will be hanged by the neck until dead, the place of execution to be the execution dock, in full view of the populace of this island . . .' "

Debrett's sharp eye, trained to tell a lumbering merchantman from a swift King's frigate as soon as its topmast cleared the horizon at sea, could make out many familiar figures grouped on the wharves and in the market square, and all staring quietly at him. He was too far to make out faces, but he knew the types: solid merchants, whores, thieves, acrobats, beggars, soldiers. They were all still, all waiting for the spectacle that the corporal, still reading from his order, and pitching his voice to carry to them across the water, was describing: " '. . . and he shall be left to hang until the carrion birds shall reduce his body to bones.' There's more like that we don't want to bother with, sir—'for the moral benefit to the people by their witnessing the execution and rotting of the body, the people thereby deriving a useful lesson in duty and obedience and a strong admonition to repentance from the heavy hand of justice so near their streets. Signed, James Durant, acting governor and acting lord chief justice.' "

Debrett noted that such of "the populace of the island" as were gathered to view the moral lesson of a man strangling to death did not seem very enthusiastic at the prospect. At the right-hand edge of the marketplace, leaning against a tavern wall, he saw Matthias, the stilt-walker, usually a capering blur in the boisterous throng, now brooding above the crowd like a resting stork. Matthias' performing monkey, James—named, Matthias was always eager to explain with total insincerity, after the Stuart pretender to the throne, and certainly not after my Lord Durant—was discernible, even at this distance, as a brown splotch on his shoulder.

Debrett sighed. Many was the coin James's nimble fingers had had of him. And now that other James, that animal aping human form, was to have his neck. And, for all the good it would do him, Debrett knew his hanging would not sit well with the Kingstonians. Willing enough to huzzah for His Majesty George I on holidays, their true loyalty lay with the buccaneers whose exploits entertained them and whose plunder enriched them. Lord Durant's execution of one of the most notorious of pirates would only deepen their distrust of any authority—and especially of the curious, tainted authority, gained by means no one was sure of, exercised with cruelty and capriciousness by Durant.

A sea breeze freshened his nostrils, and Nick Debrett glanced away from the town, toward the harbor mouth. He stiffened as his one eye, more elevated by half a head than those of the shorter men grouped around him, caught a flicker of white among the treetops. It could be a bird . . . or it could be a vagrant glimpse of a ship rounding the coast toward the harbor, screened by the forest. And if it were . . .

"*Very* good, Corporal," Major Folly said. "I don't know when I've heard an execution order delivered as movingly. You might have been a parson exhorting the rustics about tithing." The corporal looked pleased; the chaplain, murderous. "Now . . . let us proceed."

He looked expectantly at the corporal. The corporal looked hopefully at the major. "Corporal?" Folly asked, the slight quaver in his voice indicating that once again he had lost the thread of the protocol of executions and the moral lessons that went with them. The chaplain looked sourly at them both and delivered a reproachful cough.

"I believe the chaplain's turn is next, sir," the corporal said.

"Chaplain . . . yes, of course!" Folly said heartily. "Have to have one in at the death, eh? A nice prayer—a nice *short* prayer—and we can get on with the . . . ah, work. You've got something that does for pirates in your kit bag, Chaplain?"

"The Book of Common Prayer is *not* a kit bag, Major," the chaplain said. "In any case, it appears to contain no prayers for a pirate. For the King, yes . . ."

To the mind of the corporal, already partly unstrung by Folly's scornful treatment of him, this seemed to suggest that he might be at some time in the near future called upon to assist in hanging His Majesty, George I, and he broke into a sweat of apprehension.

". . . but pirates, no. I stayed up all night searching for one, but the closest I could find was something mentioning St. Peter, who, as I am sure you will recall, was a fisherman and hence involved in maritime matters . . ."

With an effort—was he a King's officer or a keeper in Bedlam, charged with the overseeing of dithering corporals and prating parsons? Folly wondered—he said, "Well, I'm sure that will do very nicely, Chaplain. Please . . . *please* go ahead."

The chaplain looked at the giant black man, and had a strong conviction that the forms and rites of the Church of England had remarkably little to do with this stoic, Cyclopean man. "Has he lived a religious life, sir?"

Debrett, tenser now as he saw the occasionally reappearing flutter of white among the far trees, drawing nearer the harbor mouth each time he glimpsed it, allowed himself a grin and rolled his eye eloquently.

Major Folly looked at the chaplain, convinced that the man's brains had finally become softened by the port he drank by the bottle, and spoke with dangerous gentleness. "No matter. He shall die a religious death. Proceed!"

Clutching his prayer book, the chaplain stood on tiptoe—which brought his mouth level with Debrett's burly shoulder—and began a quick gabbling that had at least a churchly sound. Debrett listened, unmoved, not so much from indifference to whatever spiritual consolation the chaplain might be offering as because the man's mumble was inaudible.

"Excellent!" Folly said. "As fine a prayer for a man to be hanged as I've heard." The chaplain, relieved, stopped in mid-mumble and stepped away from Debrett, who struck him as altogether too big and violent to be close to, chains or no chains.

"Now we can get on with it, Corporal," Folly said.

"Sir?" the corporal quavered.

"What . . . is . . . it?"

"We are supposed to check the trapdoor, sir."

"Then . . . test it, Corporal. Test it . . . *quickly.*" Folly closed his eyes. With this pack of louts to work with, getting even a simple execution done was like marching through a swamp in heavy boots. An officer was supposed to tell his men what to do, of course, but must he be concerned with mastering every dreary detail of procedure? Folly was perfectly prepared to risk his life for King and country by leading his men into battle, flourishing his sword; and it seemed damned unfair that he should have to puzzle over tedious matters like mastering everything about an execution. It seemed to him that there would never be an end to delays and questions and hitches, that the rising moon would find them all still in this place, with the corporal bleating his "Yes, sirs" and "No, sirs" like any sheep, working out what was to be done next, and that damned pirate still unhanged.

The corporal reached for the worn, pitted iron lever that projected from the platform and made as if to pull it. Then he looked down and observed the outline of the twin trapdoors beneath his feet.

"Bless me, sir," he said to Folly, stepping aside. "Nearly dropped *meself* through the trap, tryin' it out, and that wouldn't've done, would it, sir?"

Folly's face was unaccustomedly gentle, that of a man seeing a beautiful vision; then it hardened, and he said wearily, "No, I don't suppose it would do, Corporal."

The corporal tugged at the lever; the trap dropped with a heavy sound that echoed across the harbor. The watching crowd in the marketplace did not stir, but it seemed to Debrett that, even at that distance, he could sense a shudder sweeping through them, or perhaps it was only that his own body had involuntarily twitched at the dead thud of the dropping trap.

The doors slowly moved back into place as the

corporal, throwing his whole weight into it, pushed on the lever; a slight but ominous click told all present that they were now reset, ready for their customer.

Prodded by his escort, his mind a whirling chaos of regret and rebellion—both useless, he knew, but what was a man to do? feel nothing? sing?—Nick Debrett was urged to the center of the platform.

The soldier with the noose fastened it to the projecting beam of the gallows; in silence, he and the sergeant adjusted it around Debrett's neck. Both were careful to stand well away from the trapdoors.

The rough hemp rasped Debrett's neck, and he twitched. Yet . . . as the trees became sparser near the harbor mouth, he could see that white flutter—surely a sail now, and not a bird—more and more often, more and more clearly. Unbidden, a verse formed in his mind, complete and apt, as if written out:

Although you're consigned to the rope,
It's unmanly and idle to mope.
Until you've been topped,
It can always be stopped—
For while there is life there is hope.

"Proceed," Major Folly said grandly.

"The hood, sir." The corporal gestured at a stretch of black cloth draped over the escorting sergeant's arm.

Major Folly looked up at the sky, at Debrett—and, longingly, at the noose about the pirate's neck—and was then able to bring himself to turn to the corporal. When he spoke, it was in a voice of low, dangerous hopelessness. "Regimental tradition, Corporal, requires that all execution parties be provided with a hood, so that if the condemned man be of noble birth, he may be accorded the privilege of having his last moments, the agonies of his strangling, if you see what I mean, masked from the vulgar gaze. If you are curious, Corporal, I believe this practice dates from the Civil Wars, when this regiment was obliged to hang an earl who had fought with Cromwell and had the ill luck to be taken in the full flush of rebellion against His Martyred Majesty, without that particular nicety. Hence, lest such impoliteness occur again, we make sure that a hood is always on hand."

"I never knew that, sir," the corporal said with great interest.

"But this man is a pirate, not a prince!" Folly said, his voice rising to a near howl. "He dies bareheaded—and now!"

The corporal's hand reached for the lever once more. Then, just short of it, he stopped. "Sir?"

Debrett, tensed for the sudden drop into darkness, relaxed and drew a deep breath—one more than he had expected to take in this life.

"No more, Corporal," Folly said warningly.

The corporal looked to the foot of the platform and said, "The hangings I've been to, they always . . . just at the time, like a kind of signal, you might say . . . the drum roll, sir?"

Major Folly gave the corporal a look of purest detestation. "Let the drums sound!" And, quietly and dangerously, "Not another word, Corporal. Not one."

Like muted thunder, the drums at the foot of the gallows sounded, sending their harsh message across the waters to the sullen watchers on the docks and in the market square. Debrett could feel the solid platform vibrate to the drumming.

Once more the corporal's hand grasped the lever; once more Debrett stiffened and closed his eye.

And once again the corporal relaxed his grip. "Sir!" Moving at uncanny speed, the ship whose rigging Debrett and the corporal had seen had entered the harbor mouth and was bearing down on them—square-rigged, black of hull, sporting a fantastic figurehead of a gilded rooster with female breasts, the skull-and-crossbones flag fluttering from the masthead. Seeming to move as lightly as a trained cavalry charger, it came about and was broadside on to the fort.

Folly, still unaware of the ship's presence, opened his mouth to berate the corporal once more, but the blast of the six heavy guns aboard forestalled him. He whirled to see the craft shrouded in the smoke of the cannonade, then turned again in time to see a turret on the fort's upper embankment crumble, and gaping craters appear elsewhere on the massive walls.

"Corporal!" the major bawled over the roar of destruction.

"Yes, sir!"

"Return their fire!"

Debrett slumped with relief as the soldier took his hand from the trapdoor lever and trotted down the stairs to organize his men, followed by the two men of the escort.

Folly, imagining quite vividly the scene aboard the pirate ship as the heavy guns were rolled back, swabbed and reloaded for another punishing broadside, ground his teeth as he watched the troops unshouldering their muskets, fumbling at their belt pouches, drawing ramrods from beneath the musket barrels—what had been a precise double file of redcoats now looked like a gaggle of workmen.

"Why don't they *fire,* Corporal?"

"Muskets was unloaded, sir, as is the regulation, so as to avoid accidental firing," the corporal said, eager to be helpful in the crisis. "Being carried, as it were, for ornamentation, not use. Now, if this'd been your firing-squad execution and not a hanging, we'd have had at least some muskets loaded and primed, ready as you could wish. But what with having to load powder and ball, tamp it down, and see to the priming, it's not a matter of just snapping your fingers, as it might be, and giving the order . . ."

Folly was almost thankful when the roar of the second broadside drowned out the corporal's explanation. At closer range, only a few hundred feet now, the flying cannonballs gouged huge craters in the fortress's walls, sending rock splinters flying. He was bitterly relieved to see that the fire was aimed well above the dock—of course, the murderous rabble didn't want to risk harming their precious playmate! He made a move toward the lever the corporal had abandoned. One tug on it, and Debrett would be done with, and the pirates cheated of their goal. But . . . that was not officers' work! Once word got around that he had acted as a common hangman, he might as well turn in his commission; in every regimental mess from the Carolinas to Cawnpore he would be mockingly famous as "Choker" Folly or something equally degrading.

He clutched his sword for reassurance and scrambled down the stairs.

Still in chains and with the noose still about his neck, Nick Debrett grinned broadly as the ship loomed closer and closer to the dock. Now, beside the monstrous figurehead, he could read the name boldly painted there: *Blarney Cock.*

Major Folly saw it, too, and ground his teeth in rage. But what he saw was scarcely less infuriating than what he heard, drifting across the water from the crowd on the wharf and in the marketplace, where half of Kingston was watching a pirate vessel cannonading the fortress and a detachment of His Majesty's soldiers.

They were cheering.

Chapter 2

On the *Blarney Cock*'s deck, hard-bitten men stood by the swivcled deck carronades and prepared to add their smaller-caliber fire to the effect of the big guns' battering; others, with the swift grace born of long practice, moved about on their tasks of handling the sail lines in the intricate maneuvers the ship was performing; all grinned at the spectacle of the redcoats milling about on the dock like ants whose hill has been disarranged by a trampling foot.

Aloft, spry seamen scurried amid the rigging, adjusting sails to the shouted orders of the boatswain; from below decks came the gun captain's cry of "Fire, me lads! Fire!" and the bellow of the six heavy cannon.

Only one man seemed immune from the tension and bustle of the raid. Just aft of the gilded figurehead, a sturdy figure was squatting in concentration over the open grating known as the "head." He seemed lost in thought, and his face bore an expression of extreme concentration, as though he were working out a knotty philosophical problem.

A burly man with a face as Irish as a potato or a clay pipe roared at him, "Cinch up, Polonski, there's work to be done!"

The squatting man rose and grappled his breeches and underdrawers into place.

"No relief?" the Irishman murmured as he thrust a cutlass into Polonski's hand.

"Most of et a breeck, Moonbeam," Polonski said dourly.

Moonbeam nodded sympathetically. "Ten days without dischargin' ballast'll leave any man ready to founder. I'm thinkin' it'll take a dose o' gunpowder to clean ye out—ha! Here we are! Up ye go, lad!"

As the *Blurney Cock*'s sides grated against the dock, Polonski clawed his way up the ratlines to a point six feet above the deck; Moonbeam ran to the rail; and one agile pirate vaulted to the dock. The man looking down on the scene of ordered action from the mainmast spar smiled. In his smile, as in everything about him, there was something both winning and dangerous; it combined delight and savagery in a way that had made him known and feared by men—and known and appreciated by women—throughout the Indies.

The pirate on the dock caught the knotted end of a rope that hung from a tall freight boom at its edge, sketched a salute at Nick Debrett, still elevated on the gallow's platform, and jumped back to the deck, passing the rope's end to Moonbeam.

The Irishman swung it up to Polonski's waiting hands; others posted in the ratlines passed it up to the man poised on the topmost spar.

The soldiers, now scattering to avoid the fire from the ship, followed the rope's progress upward, and one of them, seeing the man it was meant for, gave a frightened yell: "It's Red Ned Lynch!"

Lynch called across to Debrett, pitching his voice to be heard above the rattle of small-arms fire from below, "Steady as she goes, my friend!" Debrett, grinning broadly, nodded.

Lynch wrapped the rope once about his wrist, clamped a dagger between his teeth, and leaped straight out from the spar. He seemed to soar for a moment, then plunged downward in an arc that took him nearly to the planking of the dock.

Redcoats ran as the flying apparition's booted feet came straight for their heads, heedless of Folly's bellowed instructions to "shoot the scum!" One soldier snapped off a musket shot that missed the pirate and ricocheted off a wall uncomfortably close to the major.

Lynch's carefully calculated swing landed him with a thump on the gallows platform next to Debrett. In what seemed like one motion, he spat the dagger out into his free hand, slashed the noose from around Debrett's neck, wrapped the line that had borne him from the ship about his friend's waist, and cast off.

They dropped from the platform, then, as if on the return swing of a giant pendulum, were carried past Folly and the chaplain, both gaping, past the disordered soldiers; their feet nearly scraped the dock at the foot of the freight boom; then they were over the *Blarney Cock*'s railing, above the already cheering crew, and rising toward the mainmast spar.

Their spent momentum dropped them there lightly, just as the ship's full yardage of sails was unfurled; it heeled over as it caught the wind and sped away from the dock.

Lynch steadied Debrett as they stood on the spar. "Careful, friend," he said softly. "A fall from here, weighted by those chains, and ye'd punch a hole through the deck and hull and leave us all swimming."

Debrett looked shoreward at the gallows and closed his eye for an instant. "Thank you, Ned."

The *Blarney Cock* shuddered as a final broadside sent gouts of dirt and rock dust flying from the fort's lower works and the earth embankments fronting them.

When its thunder died, Lynch and Debrett could hear the rapidly diminishing Major Folly calling on his troops to fire, then a futile popping of the muskets of the few who had managed to load and prime their weapons during the confusion.

Folly's voice, maniacal with rage, humiliation, and frustration, came to them thinly across the water. "I'll see you hang, Ned Lynch! Hear me, traitor? *And by my own hand!*"

Ned Lynch bawled back to the receding dock, "Aye, brave Major! But methinks it will have to be by a very long rope!"

The shout of laughter from the pirates on the deck below was echoed by the townspeople on Kingston's wharf and market square. Red-coated soldiers watched savagely but dared not object; the unruly throng could turn to a mob in an instant, and these Jamaicans, black and white alike, had little enough respect for the army as it was.

As a pair of strolling acrobats improvised a soaring back flip clearly derived from Lynch's daring swing to rescue Debrett, the stilt-walker's monkey looked on, squeaking and gibbering enthusiastically; and a British officer mounted his horse and made his way from the square. Once clear of it, he urged his steed to a gallop. He did not fancy what his duty required of him now: like ancient kings and tyrants, My Lord Durant could behave with singular unpleasantness toward the bearers of bad news.

Chapter 3

At the turn of the century, eighteen years before, a youthful, down-at-the-heels nobleman, younger brother to an inconsequential duke, was among the throng at King William's court witnessing the performance of the masque prepared by Mr. Dryden to observe the advent of the year 1700.

The piece was well applauded, with its elegant presentation of the gods of classical myth, but its grim ending chorus had struck home to James Durant as if it were meant for him alone.

The actor playing Momus intoned his epitaph for the departing century:

"All, all of a piece throughout . . ."

Then, pointing to the goddess Diana:

"Thy chase had a beast in view . . ."

To Mars: "Thy wars brought nothing about . . ."

To Venus: "Thy lovers were all untrue."

Then, in unison with the two-faced Janus:

" 'Tis well an old age is out,
And time to begin a new."

Durant grinned secretly. That was the truth, all right—the perfect summing up of the seventeenth century. And there was no reason to believe that the eighteenth, now upon them in a matter of minutes, would be any different.

As huntsmen, nymphs, warriors, and lovers capered on the court stage in the final dance, Durant lovingly rolled his favorite line from the masque on his lips: "Thy chase had a beast in view." Whatever Mr. Dryden had meant by it, Durant knew the beast he himself was chasing—that strange, sleek animal, cruel and lustful, that dwelt within him. He would chase that beast, but not to kill it—to capture it, tame it, train it . . . and feed it. An old age was indeed out, and he would be one of the men of the new, disdaining the tangled loyalties that had turned England upside down three times in the last hundred years, aiming only at power—not the power to rule a nation's affairs, but to enhance his own pleasure to the utmost extent.

The reigns of William and of Anne, who succeeded him early in the new century, did not afford the scope for the pleasures Lord Durant sought that the Restoration had; but on the other hand, there was less risk of losing one's head to the executioner in a political struggle. Durant made a name for himself then as a useful behind-the-scenes maneuverer—and an even more useful provider of forbidden delights to men and women in high places who shared his tastes.

When the complexities of European dynastic relationships brought the Elector of Hanover to the English throne as King George I, Durant's friends and patrons were unanimous in agreeing that it was too chancy to have the man around under the new reign—in the general turnover, there was too much likelihood that Durant's activities, and the names of those he had accommodated, would come out, to everyone's disadvantage.

"Have to do something for the fellow," one white-haired cabinet minister said through subtly rouged lips. "Preferably something far away."

Thus it was that Lord James Durant was sent out to Jamaica with an ambiguous crown commission, which he was able to use, upon the unexpected death of the royal governor—of a curious sort of indigestion occasioned by a dish he had eaten daily for ten years—to claim the post of acting governor. An attempt by Sir James Barnet, the lord chief justice of the colony, to question this in his dispatches to London, had been the only thorn in Durant's side—but this very day he had taken certain steps concerning that matter, and his power was now secure.

He luxuriated in that knowledge now as much as in the steaming water of the marble tub he lay in, and in the ministrations of the servants who tended his body—one brushing his teeth with a frayed, pungent-tasting twig, one trimming his toenails, one gently massaging his plump body.

He rotated his hips gently, feeling the soothing water wash over him in a caress gentler than the massaging fingers, and looked about the huge room. Local craftsmen had, at his direction, turned the master bedroom of a former planter's residence into a fair imitation of a Roman bath, or at least Durant's conception of one, with tall windows admitting the tropical sunlight, and with luridly colored frescoes of gods, nymphs, and satyrs doing ingenious things to and with each other; he was always particularly amused by the naïve but vivid treatment the island artist had given to Leda and the swan.

Beneath the painted walls was his living fresco—five women, seated or leaning against the walls in graceful attitudes, unmoving. Each morning, as part of his preparation for the bath, Lord Durant carefully dressed each one, from the skin outward, in what costumes he chose for the day—from the most modish contemporary dress to a filmy Roman toga—and disposed them in positions they had learned better than to alter by so much as a finger's movement. One girl, fresh to His Lordship's establishment from a Kingston brothel, had once made a natural assumption upon finding herself naked with a man clad only in an open silk robe, and had done what she felt was needed to get on with the job; now, bent and scarred, she tended the stove that kept his bathwater at the proper temperature. Lord Durant was a great appreciator of women, but in quite specific and narrow ways. . . .

The woman who lounged gracefully at the edge of the marble tub was clearly of a different order. Dark olive of complexion, with black eyes and hair, she surveyed Durant's pink, hairy form shimmering in the water with enigmatic amusement, apparently unmoved by the fact that he showed no sign of responding to the voluptuous beauty displayed by her low-cut gown. In some measure—a cast of eye, an arch of brow, nothing more definite—she seemed to some to resemble Durant, and there were whispers that she might be his cousin . . . or something closer. The normally gossipy Kingstonians were extremely wary of such speculation, however. For no reason that any of them could state clearly, all felt that any discussion of Durant's dark companion would be unhealthy.

The touch of servile fingers, the scent of perfumed steam rising from the water, the taste of the spice twig darting among his teeth, the sight of the well-proportioned room with its paintings and living statues, pleased four of Lord Durant's senses to perfection; not the most decadent of ancient Romans might have enjoyed more. It was a source of regret to him that even the most devoted of antiquaries had not been able to discover what mode of music the Romans had used; though his personal idol, the Emperor Nero, was said to have fiddled while Rome burned, the tune he had played was beyond conjecture. However, the butterfly-light strains of Scarlatti emanating from the lute now being played would do quite well enough. . . . Durant raised his head slightly to look at the lute player, who sat on a low stool a short distance from the tub—a delicately built young man with long, fair hair. He was gazing in Durant's direction, but in a manner so unfocused that he might have been seeing anything or nothing as his long, tapering fingers plucked the strings of his instrument.

Seeing the direction of Durant's look, the dark woman by his side reached down and slowly ran the tip of one pointed fingernail from his chest to his thigh in a single graceful movement, then withdrew her hand and resumed her placid pose; Durant shot her a quick glance and lay back once again.

A door in the far wall of the room opened, admitting a tall, darkly handsome young man—like all of Durant's entourage, of striking appearance—who strode toward the tub. By the time he reached it, the last trace of the smile with which he had entered—prompted by the breathless army officer's obvious relief at not having to deliver his message to Durant in person—had vanished, and his face was businesslike and grave.

"Your pardon, M'Lord," he said, standing at the tub's edge. Durant's eyes narrowed. He had no doubt of Willard Culverwell's efficiency as a secretary, and no reason to suspect his loyalty, but there was sometimes something in his manner that rankled. Though he was as respectful as any servant approaching a powerful master, there was a nuance in his attitude that made Durant painfully and momentarily aware of being a naked middle-aged man floating in several gallons of warm water, rather than an antique sybarite cultivating his civilized senses to the fullest. No matter; he had plans for Willard. The lad with the lute had once showed that spark of disapproving individuality, but Durant had broken him of that and trained him to a more rewarding viewpoint. . . .

"You ask my pardon; whether I shall grant it depends on what your reason is for interrupting my ablutions," he said, striving for a menacing playfulness.

"The pirate Debrett, M'Lord . . ."

"Ah, yes—that popinjay Folly has hanged him, has he?"

"Not quite, M'Lord."

Durant's face reddened. "Not *quite!* How do you half-hang a man?"

"At the moment of the proposed execution, sir," Willard Culverwell said woodenly, keeping a grave countenance only by dint of biting quite hard on the inside of his cheek, "a ship appeared, cannonaded the fortress, and made off with the prisoner."

As though one of the electric eels lately discovered in the Spanish colonies had been dropped into the tub with him, Lord Durant gave a spasmodic jerk that sent a wave of bathwater to drench the man who had been trimming his toenails. The pedicurist quickly turned his grimace of shock and displeasure into a sickly smile, as though being slopped by Lord Durant were the height of pleasure—those who served him had learned that it was generally safer to take anything My Lord might do in that manner.

"That stupid, stupid, blundering fool!" Durant shrilled. "I entrust the man with the responsibility of a simple execution, something the merest child could undertake, and how does he show his gratitude? By losing the prisoner altogether! And the rescuer was . . .?

"The pirate Lynch, sir—Red Ned, as he is known."

"Of course, it would be Lynch! Damn his common soul!"

Culverwell nodded solemnly, with just that extra edge of overdone agreement that sat so poorly with Durant. The acting royal governor and acting lord chief justice slammed his plump fist against the edge of the tub.

"Culverwell," he hissed, as nearly as he could come to hissing a name entirely lacking in S's, "you will deliver a message to Major Folly. You will tell him that one more blunder, one more *folly,* major or minor, and he will be on the next ship to England—in chains!"

"Very good, M'Lord." Willard Culverwell's respectful demeanor was mingled with the slightest tinge of enthusiasm; it was his opinion, which he tried to keep prudently concealed, that Major Folly would be vastly improved by a felon's fetters.

Yet, there are fetters and fetters—or rather, the fettered and the fettered; it depends on who bears them. Culverwell, who had only a second ago been savoring the thought of Major Folly loaded down with chains, now saw the matter quite differently as he looked out the tall window and saw an elderly, distinguished man, manacled at arms and legs, being hustled up the front stairway of Lord Durant's mansion.

He turned back to address Durant in bewilderment. "Sir, it's James Barnet, the Lord Chief Justice. In *chains,* sir?"

Durant ran his fingers down his hairy pink chest, letting them quiver like questing, fleshy fish. "The *former* Lord Chief Justice, my good Culverwell. We happen to have discovered that Sir James Barnet cherishes treasonable sentiments of affection for the cause of the pretender—that *other* James, the Stuart scion who lurks in the court of Louis of France, awaiting his chance to overset our good King George."

Culverwell was bewildered. "Sir James a Jacobite conspirator?"

Durant shrugged, sending a wave splashing near the edge of the tub. "His daughter spent ten years at school in Paris, where the Pretender maintains his travesty of a court, and sounds like a damned Frenchy herself; it may not be true that Barnet is a sympathizer, but the wench's stay there makes it plausible, at least for the moment. In these matters of politics, my dear Culverwell, the great thing is to be able to accuse convincingly, not to prove one's case. Now, have Barnet brought up for his audience—I rather fancy the *salle d'armes* for that."

He waved a hand in languid dismissal, and Culverwell turned abruptly and strode out. Durant snapped his fingers in the face of one of the attendants. "Enough. Prepare me."

The dark lady smiled as solicitous hands raised Durant's steaming pink body from the tub and with slavish tenderness began patting it dry.

In addition to cultivating and indulging his senses, Lord Durant believed strongly in training his body and developing its skills, for without a keenly maintained physique, sensual pleasure could not be fully appreciated. Hence his *salle d'armes* was more than a room set aside for practicing swordplay; a vaulting horse, parallel bars, weights, and a pair of rings dangling from ropes showed that gymnastic exercises worthy of a devoted athlete were part of its function. The whole effect might have been pleasingly healthy if it had not been for the blood-red carpet on the floor and the excessive number of full-length mirrors lining the wall.

As Sir James Barnet was led in by two guards, Durant was indulging in one of his favorite pastimes, fencing with three opponents at once, skilled black swordsmen whose slashing lunges and cuts he parried with lightning speed and savagery. As always, Durant and his opponents fenced with naked blades; he disdained the protective button on the *épée*'s tip, needing the prospect of bloodshed to bring out his fullest skill.

The rattle and clank of Barnet's chains distracted one swordsman's attention for an instant, and he flicked his glance toward the door, where the elderly man stood between two impassive soldiers. Durant's blade darted past his guard, and its tip raked the black man's chest, leaving a bright line of red welling up.

"Here is where your attention must be!" Durant said sharply, flourishing his sword. "Here! Right here!"

The wounded man nodded silently and resumed his share of the swordplay. The dark lady, seated on a richly upholstered chair in the corner of the room, smiled; the tip of her tongue darted out and retreated with a quick, catlike flick, as if tasting something succulent on her gently curved, full lips. The youthful lute player also regarded the scene, but with his usual distant gaze that made it questionable whether he was actually seeing what was taking place.

Sir James Barnet looked with bewilderment and disgust at the grotesque ballet being performed in the center of the room, and repeated to infinity in the mirrors lining it.

"Sir James, how good of you to come," Durant called out mockingly, driving his three opponents back with a series of thrusts and lunges. "You will excuse me, I trust, if I continue with my practice while we speak. I have *so* little time for the pleasures in life. You'll understand, I'm sure."

Futilely, Sir James strained at the chains binding his wrists, and made no reply.

"I trust," Durant said, evading a concerted assault by two of his opponents, "that you are not suffering a great deal of discomfort, Sir James?"

Barnet's voice was strong and harsh. "Is that why you had me removed from my house and brought here in chains? To inquire as to whether they are of a proper fit?"

"I have never really thought of myself as a *cruel*

man," Durant said with a smile of dazzling sweetness, "only a clever one."

"Indeed you are, Lord Durant. But not clever enough to deceive the people of Kingston. The *people,* Durant, not your lackeys and hired assassins!"

Durant's blade scythed back and forth as he answered, "Your first statement was the correct one, Sir James: I am clever enough to accomplish what I propose to . . . Be wary! Be wary!"

This shrilled admonition was addressed not to Sir James Barnet but to one of the two unwounded swordsmen, whose guard Durant had suddenly penetrated; he followed it with a leaping lunge that slashed the man across the face.

"Poor, *poor* Keyo," Durant purred as the man stepped back and wiped the welling blood away. "Alas, your ebon cheek now sports a scar. But never mind, it suits you well. *En garde!*"

The three swordsmen regrouped and fatalistically began their all-too-realistic fencing practice with their master and tormentor. "You must understand, Sir James," Durant said as he parried their attacks, speaking as effortlessly as if reclining in a drawing-room chair instead of bounding and darting about the floor with edged steel flickering in front of his face, "that you are merely a pawn. A rebellious one, to be sure, but a pawn all the same. And for the time being, to suit my purposes, I am forced to remove you from the playing board. A few months, Sir James, that's all the time I'll need. And your silence during that time."

"To rape the people," Barnet said grimly.

Durant, still moving with swift and lethal grace, smiled as though he rather liked the image. "That is a very *harsh* description. I prefer to think of it as . . . payment due."

"Payment for what?"

Durant's face twisted as he recalled the boots he had licked and the degrading services he had performed for the rich and powerful to make his way in the world —but not even to a helpless old man, totally in his power, would he reveal those. Some secrets in his life were only for the dark woman who shared that life; any other to whom Lord Durant revealed himself fully could count his remaining lifetime in moments. And, just now, it did not suit his plans to have Sir James Barnet killed. He resorted to cynical bluster. "For the years I've suffered on these filthy islands, and for the interminable hours I've had to endure such righteous, insufferable bores as yourself, Sir James."

Barnet looked at the capering, yet deadly, epicene nobleman—the idea that such a creature could by the fact of his birth be counted honorable came close to making Sir James regret that Cromwell's Commonwealth had not, after all, prevailed—and almost spat out his distaste. "All that is insufferable, Lord Durant, is you. And my only failure has been in not being able to expose you and all the wickedness you represent. Were the governor still alive—"

"Alas"—another series of brilliant parries and ripostes drove back the advancing black swordsmen—the Governor still alive—"

"An extraordinary convenience for you, Lord Durant. But hear this, sir: as surely as I stand before you now, others will come, and you shall not succeed, but die—and men will dance on your grave!"

For a moment, in that lurid, sickly room, the balance of things seemed to alter. A chained, helpless old man snarled his defiance, and the one unwounded swordsman, seeing that Durant was paying more attention to his prisoner than his opponents, slipped through his guard and drew blood from his shoulder.

Durant drew in a short, hissing breath and stepped back, his swiftly moving blade once more guarding him effectively. His cold glance measured the man who had cut him, and he gave an almost imperceptible nod of decision. The black man facing him returned his look as coolly; he had read his fate in the Englishman's eyes and was prepared to accept it.

Durant's swordplay increased in intensity and brilliance as he went on speaking to Barnet, and his voice grew higher and more strained. "You are not in a position to make threats, Sir James!"

"Unlock these chains, and I will do far more than threaten!"

"You will do *nothing* but what I direct you to do. I have become weary of this debate, and tired of the sight of you, and my final words are these: all your lands and property are herewith forfeit to the Crown—which I have the honor to represent in this colony. Your dear wife and charming daughter can find themselves a new home in whatever slum appeals to them. And you, my dear Sir James, shall be removed at once to the fortress, and there you shall be made to serve a sentence for what length of time suits my *pleasure!*"

On the last word, Durant's voice rose to a screech, and with an eerie, apelike bound, he dived past the flickering blades of the two men he had marked with his own and ran the third man through the abdomen.

Barnet heard the choked death scream, the thud of the swordsman's corpse on the carpeted floor, and the ecstatic rasp of Durant's breathing as he stood back, holding the bloodied *épée*. He looked around the room at the sickened faces of the women posed against the wall, the young musician, still staring blankly, and the enigmatic visage of the dark woman, who seemed to be regarding Durant and the dead man in front of him with much the same detached interest. As Lord Chief Justice, charged with keeping the King's peace among a volatile people, Sir James Barnet had encountered much crime, violence, and assorted wrongdoing, but never before had he been aware of being in the presence of ultimate evil.

Chapter 4

Whatever their feelings about other aspects of the military life, soldiers of all nations tend to delight in the chance of a nice bit of looting; at no time in history has standard government pay been so generous that the men of any army could afford to ignore whatever pickings lay around. Thus the troops busily engaged in stripping the elegant country house of Sir James Barnet of its furnishings, paintings, silverware, carpeting, bric-a-brac—of everything, in short, but the paint on the walls—might have been expected to be exultant. They were, however, doing their work with as little joy as hired porters engaged to remove a householder's belongings from one residence to another; and that was what, in effect, they were doing. All that was being hauled, handed, or thrown from the Barnet house was to go to another, that of Lord Durant, with none of it falling to the lot of the soldiers actually doing the looting.

One private fancied a miniature, painted in bright colors on ivory, of a lady in a low-cut dress of the Restoration period, fifty years before; it was not the artistry of the portrait that attracted him so much as the gold setting and the notable amount of bosom the lady was complacently displaying. "Might've been one of these here royal favorites," he said to a companion. "One of King Charles's lights-o'-love, that got made a duchess along of being bedded by the old wencher. Wonder what it'd fetch in the marketplace?"

"Fetch a crowd to watch you bein' flogged," the other soldier said. "Durant's got eyes and ears all over, and you can count on it that anything that sticks to your fingers out o' this lot will burn 'em."

The soldier with the miniature dropped it hastily into the sack the other was holding.

At the front veranda of the house, a double file of soldiers stood between the entrance and a small, smart coach that stood in the crushed-shell drive, forming a corridor through which Major Folly was escorting two women, each carrying a small valise.

The elder, handsome but gaunt with shock and worry over her vanished husband, winced as she saw the antlike scurrying of the soldiers who were carrying away the belongings acquired over a lifetime to waiting freight wagons. The breathtaking brunette beauty of the younger was marred by an expression of frozen rage and the smudges of a dried tearstain. In her years in Paris, Jane Barnet had seen strange and appalling things, but nothing so shocking as this looting of a British judge's residence by British troops.

As the women silently approached the coach, Folly nodded at the corporal who stood by it, determinedly ignoring the savage glare of the Barnets' black servant stationed next to him. The corporal snapped to attention and intercepted Lady Barnet.

"I will have to examine your bags, ma'am."

Lady Barnet roused herself from her shock and turned on him the sort of glance that in better days had been able to freeze an impertinent guest to his chair. "You will do nothing of the kind."

"I have my orders, ma'am."

"Damn your orders!"

The corporal blinked and looked aggrieved. Ladies ought not to talk like that—and certainly ought not to give a poor soldier trouble in going about his duty. It was bad enough doing your best to hang a pirate and then getting a wigging for it afterward for something that wasn't your fault. . . . He looked hopefully toward the major, who might be used to this sort of thing.

Folly stepped forward and came up behind the

women, neither of whom acknowledged his presence. He smiled crookedly and said, "I apologize for the inconvenience, but it *will* be necessary for you to do as requested."

He reached for Lady Barnet's bag. Jane Barnet's full skirt rustled as she turned and looked up at him, her hand moving in a quick gesture that her mother's presence masked from the attendant soldiers.

Folly, his hand on the handle of Lady Barnet's valise, looked down and froze. Jane Barnet's knuckles showed white around the handle of a short but keen dagger, poised almost between the legs of his tight white uniform trousers. Her voice was low, pitched only for his ears, but neither its quietness nor the French accent with which her years in Paris had overlaid her English masked the menace of her message: "I will cut them off if you persist."

A twitch of the dagger removed any doubt about what "they" were, and Folly turned pale, then smiled sickly. "However," he said heartily to the corporal, "I think it would be safe to assume that Lady Barnet and her daughter would not attempt to deceive us by secreting a valuable cargo within their valises. Don't you agree, Corporal?"

"Well, sir, assuming is all very well, I expect, but the orders was specific about—"

As Folly felt the pressure of the dagger on his inner thigh, he almost shouted, "I said, *you agree,* do you not?"

"Certainly, sir," the corporal said, offended.

"Right, then! Let the women pass, and let the coach leave unmolested." He exhaled in relief as the blade was withdrawn and slipped away in its hiding place in Jane Barnet's dress. Of course, she probably *wouldn't* have . . . Then he remembered the single glance she had darted at him as she spoke, and decided that she *would.* The women out here really had no sense of decorum.

The vexed corporal stepped aside, and the servant handed the two women into the coach, then mounted the elevated driver's seat and cracked the reins. As the horse tugged at the traces and the coach's wheels began to turn, Major Folly had a last glimpse of Jane Barnet's face looking from the window. She did not seem to be giving a lingering glance at her former home, but rather to be studying his face, as if she wanted to be sure she would know it again, anywhere.

He made a formal, mocking bow to the departing coach, then straightened. The day was hot and his stiff uniform heavy, but the memory of Jane Barnet's expression—and of her dagger—left him with a chill feeling.

He turned and saw the corporal once again at work, directing two soldiers lugging a heavy, iron-bound chest toward one of the wagons.

Major Folly ground his teeth in exasperation. One moment the fellow was blathering about how specific the orders had been, the next he was forgetting one of the most specific of all. Lord Durant had been very clear about taking no chances with Sir James Barnet's family treasures—and that chest was worth as much as the rest of the contents of the house put together.

"Not there, fools!" he called. He pointed to a large coach, drawn by a four-horse team, farther down the drive. "There! In my coach!"

He watched sharply as the corporal saluted and ordered the soldiers with the chest to change direction.

A hundred yards away, screened by a clump of trees, another man, mounted on a horse, watched with equal interest. There'd be no mistaking that coach when the time came. . . . Willard Culverwell gave a somber look at the empty Barnet house, and his face hardened. He slipped from his horse and began bringing out a variety of implements from his saddlebags. The first was a crossbow—silent and accurate, in many ways a more efficient killer than the musket that had supplanted it in warfare. Culverwell lifted the heavy weapon to his cheek and sighted on the strutting figure of Folly; it would be an easy shot. He sighed and laid the crossbow on the grass. Much as he would like to see Folly transfixed by an arrow, that was not what he was here for; he'd better get about his mission.

"There was a young virgin from Malta
Who swooned on the boat to Gibraltar.
Though she lost her virginity
In that vicinity,
She still ended up at the altar."

Ned Lynch's voice rose lazily in the clear air as he finished reciting his latest composition. He lay on his back, looking up at the bright sky, supremely content. With his ship at anchor in the cove below, his friend Nick Debrett by his side, and the prospect of action—and profit—imminent, he felt the need of nothing more.

Nick Debrett nodded his appreciation at Ned's limerick, stared up at the sky for a moment, and essayed his own:

"There was a young lady named Starkie
Who had an affair with a darky.
The result of her sins
Was quadruplets, not twins—
One black, one white, and two khaki."

Lynch shrugged. "A fair effort, Nick. Not outstanding, but fair. Now, how about this?

"I asked myself, Nick, will I make her?
In the morning, I just couldn't wake her.
So I sauntered away
And spent the whole day
With another young girl in Jamaica."

"Not one of your best, Ned," Debrett said solemnly. "Now, you know, I did one I liked pretty well yesterday." He recited the verse he had composed as he waited to be hanged on Execution Dock.

"That was cool work," Ned Lynch said. "Almost a pity they didn't hang you, so you could have had a chance to use it."

Debrett grinned. "It may come in handy yet. In this trade, you've every chance to rise in the world, especially at the end of a noose."

"Well, it could come to that, but you've got the right end of it; the thing to be sure of is that you go out in style. I always did think that, since I was a lad." Lynch was suddenly thoughtful, as his mind roamed the past and once again went over the road that had led him from the green hills and fields of Ireland to the more vividly green tropics.

"You know, when I was a boy, I found in a book that there was a man, an English nobleman, beheaded in London the day I was born, and I got to be curious about that and read about him. Lord Russell, his name was, and he'd done something against the King or his brother, who was the next King—a little beforehand, he was, but not much, for just about everybody was against the new King in a few years, and chased him away to France. Anyhow, they took his head off in the Tower, this Lord Russell, and there was a story they told that stuck in my mind. The day before he was to be killed, he had a nosebleed, and the doctor came for it, and Russell says that he wouldn't have blood let to cure it as they did then—that would be seen to tomorrow. Now, don't you know, that struck me—a man that was to die in that terrible way, and able to make a good joke about it."

Debrett was dubious. "Might have been better, if he was that clever, to figure out a way to have stayed alive."

Ned Lynch guffawed. "Dear man, are you holding yourself up as a model of caution to me now? Why, I've seen you take risks that made my own blood run cold, which it's not much inclined to do."

"Only when I had to or I saw a good chance of bringing it off," Debrett said firmly. "I'll fight for what I want, and hazard my neck when it comes to that, but only if the prize is worth it."

"Then," Lynch said thoughtfully, "you've not done foolish and brave and wicked things just for the glory of it, as you might say—to prove yourself a man, say, or to have a bit of fun?"

"Never. I was a slave, and did what I had to to get out of that. I was ignorant and did what I had to to get out of that. And I was poor, and I'm doing what I have to about that, too. Of course"—He grinned briefly—"there's nothing says I can't enjoy some of it along the way."

"Hm." Lynch was a little disconcerted. In the years he had sailed—and plundered, caroused, and wenched—with Nick Debrett, he had considered him a kindred spirit; what else would Red Ned Lynch's best friend be but another such as himself? But he saw now that he and Debrett had come to their present places in life by different ways and for different reasons, and that, for all their closeness, they were different people. It struck him that he had never wondered much about what people were like and why they did whatever they did; he took them as they were, and dealt with them as friend or foe, as the occasion demanded. And he realized that that was how he had treated himself as well; it had never occurred to him to wonder why he was what he was, instead of something else entirely, or why he had done the things he had done. . . .

Charles II, who had Lord Russell escorted from this life on the same day that Edward Patrick Lynch entered it, died within two years, leaving his widely detested brother as King. Ned Lynch was five, and completely unconcerned, when James II was ousted in the "Glorious Revolution" of 1688 and retired to France and the sober Dutchman William of Orange became King of England. Young Ned Lynch would have done well to be concerned, for James's flight from the throne, and his son's attempt to regain it, were to be largely responsible for transforming an Irish squire's son with prospects of a comfortable if uneventful life into the most feared pirate in the Indies.

Ned's father had prospered enough to send him for a gentlemanly finishing to Trinity College in Dublin; but the students he gravitated to were not the sporting set who snored through their lectures, but certain firebrands to whom William seemed another Cromwell, embodiment of English domination and Ireland's shame and slavery. When the inept and disliked ex-King, who had had the good sense at least to stay out of plots to restore him, in spite of his wife's intriguing, died in exile, Ned Lynch's associates thrilled at the recognition of his son as James III, rightful King of England—by the kings of France and Spain, the Duke of Savoy, and the Pope. They chose to ignore the fact that the English did not see it that way, and, as Queen Anne succeeded the early-dead William and continued his enmity toward Louis of France, protector and patron of "James III," planned direct action.

"Wild geese, we called ourselves," Ned Lynch reminisced to Nick Debrett on that bright tropical hillside so many years after. "Young Irishmen, slipping away to fight for King Louis and King James against Queen Anne and the Duke of Marlborough. There was an emperor into it, that the fight was supposed to be about, but we never paid that any attention. We dodged the Queen's men that was on the lookout for such as us, and sailed for Holland. I remember, that was the first time I sailed, and it got to me, being out in the open water. And there was a song one of the sailors made up, that stuck with me. . . ."

His mind drifted back across the intervening fifteen years—no, more than that, now—to the frail but heavy-laden craft wallowing in the Channel mists, and the soft country voice singing:

. . . Twenty young wild geese, ready set to fly,
Sailing for the Lowlands low.
The Lowlands low, the Lowlands low, sailing for
the Lowlands low.

These twenty wild geese gave Queen Anne the slip,
Sailing for Louis in Flanders.
He and Jack Malbrook both are in the grip,
Fighting in the Lowlands low . . .

Young Ned Lynch and his Wild Geese companions arrived in Holland just at the time "Jack Malbrook"—John Churchill, Duke of Marlborough—was made Generalissimo of the Imperial Armies, and Lynch himself had a brush with possible glory, when, as the armies broke up for the year—civilized warfare being impossible in the winter mud of Flanders—he and a ragtag body of local partisans nearly captured the Duke in an ambush.

The next months and years slipped by more rapidly than he would have thought possible, in the futile exercises of a military camp, in the dull but dangerous business of guard duty at the court of the self-styled King in exile—the Pretender, as even his partisans now called him. Somewhere along the line, young (but not so young as he had been) Ned Lynch lost the amalgam of idealism, loyalty, and patriotism that had made him a Wild Goose—a name he was beginning to think more appropriate as each month passed—through seeing something of the nature of nations and armies and the men who ruled them. Yet, he had pledged himself, and so he stayed.

The slaughter at the Battle of Ramillies, which should have been decisive against the Pretender's cause, was nearly so for Ned Lynch. Two things impressed him—that he was not afraid in the heat of battle, and that it seemed a damned foolish business to risk his neck for men and causes he did not give a tinker's dam for.

When, in 1707, Major Edward Lynch sailed with the Pretender's forces on the *Salisbury*, he did so under the impression that he had no illusions about it: if the landing at Edinburgh were successful, and James made King, the officers who had helped him would then be free to help themselves—at least, that was how it had worked when Charles II returned to the throne forty years before. But he had been operating under one significant illusion—that the Pretender's invasion had a chance of succeeding. When the *Salisbury* was captured, and he and the other Scotch and Irish officers in James's service were taken to London and quartered in the Tower and Newgate, Ned Lynch perceived his error.

Fortunately, he was not of grand enough standing to rate incarceration in the Tower of London, where his admired Lord Russell had been imprisoned and executed. The brawling precincts of Newgate were less well guarded, and Ned Lynch was out of them and on the streets of London within a week of his arrival there, having bribed a guard with good French gold to list him as among the daily dead so that no pursuit might follow.

Wary and on his own in the biggest city he had ever seen, Lynch wondered what to do with himself. The Pretender, and his son Charles after him, might go on chasing their dreams of becoming kings in England, but that was nothing to do with Ned Lynch. He'd spent five years of his life on that dream, and it seemed wasted now. He found the Londoners much like the Irish, and like men everywhere—and women, too, though the London ones seemed to have learned a lot more than their Dublin sisters—and to kill and be killed over the question of whether a Scot or a German should rule either or both peoples seemed the sheerest lunacy.

Lounging in White's Coffee-House and perusing the newspapers that the management provided for its patrons, Lynch was aware of being at a loose end. He had enough money for a month or so, but no trade, and little desire to return home; all he knew was some of the dodges of warfare, and how to survive the intrigues and dangers of court and camp.

Then he stiffened in his chair. An item in the newspaper, a story he had glanced at and passed over, now struck him as suddenly significant. Something about new naval regulations. . . . He turned back and found it, reread it, and grinned.

The Admiralty had set out regulations for the distribution of "prizes" in fixed proportions among the officers and men of the Royal Navy—that is, whatever the value of enemy warships or cargo ships they might capture, a percentage of it would be paid each man according to his rank. " 'Twill encourage the brave seamen to hunt out fat merchantmen rather than risking their necks against a Frenchy man-o'-war," Lynch murmured, marshaling his thoughts. "And from that, I'd think it'd be but a short step for some of them to turn pirate outright. And now one thinks of it, isn't that a grand life for a fellow such as myself? It's a way of using what I know how to do, and for my own benefit instead of the Pretender's or the Queen's or some such. . . ." Of course, it was against the law, and a hanging matter at that—but it was hard to tell the difference between criminal piracy and what the Admiralty was encouraging, if you looked at it closely. . . .

Within a year, Lynch was in Barbados, where he soon found his way into the crew of a pirate vessel. His dash, and his professional acquaintance with military tactics, including the all-important art of gunnery, soon elevated him to first mate of the *Golden Griffin;* and a fatal disagreement with Tench, the ship's captain, over the honesty of the division of spoils, made him heir to the ship and captain of it in his own right. Lynch signalized the change of regime—which had been accomplished with no less justice and far less bloodshed than most political changes in the world—by renaming the ship the *Blarney Cock*. The rooster-headed, woman-chested gilt figurehead had always struck him as ridiculous, and it was easier to change the name to fit that notion than to commission a new figurehead.

Nick Debrett, new to piracy but already a boon companion of the new captain's, demurred. "Won't a name like that be taken as a joke?"

Lynch grinned briefly. "Not after tomorrow." And it was true that, after the next day's raid on Cartagena, which left two Spanish warships sinking and a treasure galleon stripped, the *Blarney Cock* was treated with deadly seriousness throughout the waters of the Spanish Main.

And now, years later, it was still there, uncaptured and unsunk, lying at rest in the waters of the cove, manned by a crew more efficient and ruthless—and loyal—than that of any naval vessel in the world.

With a start, Ned Lynch brought himself back to the present. Nick Debrett was starting another verse: "There was a young girl whose frigidity . . ." when Lynch's upraised hand stopped him. "What, Ned?"

Lynch crouched and set one ear to the ground. "I think I feel a trembling beneath my spine. A coach and two horses, fast approaching. No . . . four horses. Black ones. No . . . it's as you had it in your wee verse, 'One black, one white, and two khaki.' "

Nick Debrett grinned. "You feel the worms, Ned, only the worms. We've not had the signal yet."

Lynch rolled over on his back and blew the seeds from a dandelion, watching them drift away in the light air. "You know what your trouble is, Nick? You lack a sense of romance, of the lure of bright eyes and rosy thighs."

"Possibly so. But I have a fine sense of gold, my friend, and it's the yellow stuff we're after today, not the pink."

Lynch lay back, a little nettled. Debrett was getting to be a sobersides, with no fun to him. Soon he'd be practicing piracy with all the joylessness of a merchant on the London 'Change. He wanted gingering up a bit, so he did. An idea came to Lynch, and he sat upright, his eyes alight.

"What think you of a small sporting wager, Nick?"

"Now?"

"Aye, now. A race. And the loser pays . . . what? Two doubloons? Four? Ah, make it worth our while—say, six doubloons!" He jumped to his feet, excited by the prospect.

Nick Debrett closed his one eye and shook his head. "Oh, my. What we've got to do, and the plunder we'll get from it, isn't enough for you—you have to make bets on it as well. And have you already forgotten the last time we raced?"

Ned Lynch paced back and forth, cheerful and exhilarated. This was something like it, now—danger, riches, and the chance to stir up his friend's sense of adventure. "Forgotten? I won! By a finger's breadth!"

"*I* won," Debrett said severely. "By a hair's breadth."

Ned Lynch shrugged. "Ah, well, *one* of us won."

His savagely merry blue eyes looked hard at Debrett, who, in spite of his expressed reservations, was tickled by the idea. After a pause, the black man said, "Six doubloons?"

"Six it is."

"You'll pay?"

Lynch drew himself up in mock indignation at this slur on his probity as a sportsman. "If I lose," he said grandly.

"When you lose."

Ned Lynch thrust his hand out; Nick Debrett clasped it, sealing the wager, and both men grinned in delight.

"We'll start at the signal, then?" Debrett said.

Ned Lynch nodded. "And the devil take the hindmost."

Debrett looked down the sloping hill, with lanes and trails barely traceable among the banana palms and other trees. "I'd say he'd have a chance at the foremost as well, Ned—one false step, and our friend the major won't have to worry about breaking our necks on the gallows."

Such considerations were far from Ned Lynch's mind, and he shrugged. Whatever his fate, he was sure it was not to crack his skull open on a Jamaican rock. "The lobsterbacks'll have had all the time they need for their brave work by now. We should have the signal any minute, I'd think."

Willard Culverwell had everything in readiness: the crossbow was cocked, its steel arms winched back as far as they would go; a shaft lay in the firing trough, with a gray paper cylinder from which a two-inch fuse protruded attached to it.

He peered through the concealing screen of foliage. The freight wagons, loaded with the Barnets' possessions, were gone. Now Folly was ordering two soldiers up to the outside driver's seat of his coach, into which the chest had been loaded; now he was climbing inside the coach; now the four horses set off at a gallop down the drive.

Culverwell pulled a tinderbox from his pocket and held a flint to it. Everything depended on whether the coach took the route he had predicted; if it turned left at the end of the drive, the whole plan would have been in vain.

The vehicle paused as it approached the dusty highway . . . then turned right. Willard Culverwell grinned savagely, struck flint to the tinderbox, and ignited the gray cylinder's fuse. It spat sparks, and he lifted the crossbow to his shoulder, aimed it straight up, and fired.

Half a mile away, relaxed but poised for action, Ned Lynch and Nick Debrett could not see the crossbow bolt rising in the air, but the flash of light halfway toward the zenith, followed seconds later by a light *crump,* told them that Willard Culverwell's signal bomb had worked—and that their hastily wagered-on race must now begin.

A deerlike spring down the hillside started each on his way. The slope was clear for a hundred yards; then the trees and undergrowth began. Each chose his own path, making lightning decisions to veer to left or right, crash through a tangle of vines or sidestep it, leap over a log or stone. They nearly cannoned into each other where two trails converged, and for a moment ran steadily side by side.

" 'There was a young girl whose frigidity . . .'?" Lynch prompted Debrett, reminding him of the unfinished limerick.

"That's right," Debrett said, not quite panting, but taking care to speak on the exhalation of the deep breaths his exertion required. "Go on with it, if you can."

"Ah . . . 'Approached cateleptic rigidity . . .' " By God, he'd fetched up "cataleptic" from some dull lecture at Trinity, half a lifetime ago—who said there was nothing to be gained from education? They were past the trees now, and approaching a pasture rimmed by a stone wall. Like a pair of matched thoroughbreds, they leaped it in unison and raced across the flat, fertile compound. Debrett ran with grim concentration, feet pounding hard; Lynch moved more lightly, seemingly almost effortlessly, like a man indulging in his favorite game and enjoying it mightily; yet both made precisely the same speed, neither one's style giving any advantage.

Apparently some of Debrett's concentration had gone toward literary rather than athletic goals, for he suddenly murmured, in cadence to his strides, " ' 'Til you gave her a drink, when she quickly would sink . . .' "

He threw a quick sidelong glance to Lynch, who gave a laugh of delight at the new lines—at the same time noticing and leaping over a fresh pile of cattle droppings. Debrett paid for taking his eye off the route by stepping squarely into another such pile, fouling one boot and breeches leg as the force of his stride caused it to erupt—and gave Lynch the inspiration for the final line: " 'In a state of complaisant liquidity'!"

The mishap made Debrett break stride and give vent to a quick, pungent curse on all cows and their digestive systems. Lynch, now half a pace ahead, roared with laughter and called, "Mustn't tarry, Nick!"

Debrett put on a burst of speed, and was once again level with Ned Lynch as they reached and vaulted over the far wall of the pasture and onto the dirt road that ran beyond it, slowing only a little as they turned left and raced down the road, their pounding feet raising clouds of dust.

They could not see the intersection with the highway, which was screened by trees; but by the same token, the occupants of the coach, whose approach could now be deduced from the thunder of sixteen hooves, the creaking of harness, and the rumble of quickly turning wheels, could not see them.

Chapter 5

The sound of the approaching coach growing louder in their ears, Debrett and Lynch pounded down the road toward where it angled into the highway. Major Folly's coach had made better time from the Barnet house than they had anticipated, and their race with each other had now become a grim necessity rather than a sporting matter.

The space between the highway and the road the two pirates were on narrowed down to a point where they met; the instant before Ned Lynch and Nick Debrett reached that point, four horses galloped past it, drawing the heavy coach behind them. Its speed, and the cloud of dust thrown up by the horses, obscured the running men from the inattentive gaze of the soldiers on the box.

Even as he prepared to draw on his deepest reserves of strength to overhaul the speeding coach, Ned Lynch was able to note with delight that it was drawn by a pair of matched bays and one coal-black and one shimmering white horse—"One white, one black, and two khaki," just the way he'd jokingly predicted!

He closed the gap between himself and the coach, inch by inch, feeling the exultation of his primitive ancestors, who, in the days before horses and guns, would run down the deer they hunted. An eerie cry from close behind him made him break stride. To his astonishment, Nick Debrett, a crucial few feet behind when they burst onto the highway, was now level with him . . . and now ahead!

Dust clogging their eyes and rasping in their lungs, both men drew up to the rear of the coach. By less than a heartbeat, Debrett's fingers were the first to close on its undercarriage.

They drew themselves onto the heavily sprung framework, the wheels rattling next to their heads, and the body of the carriage swaying and jouncing on its springs, threatening every second to slam into them. They lay there, gasping for breath, coated with road dust so that they looked like two men made of dried mud.

After a moment they were able to raise their heads and grin at each other. "One white, one black, and two khaki," Debrett muttered, mouthing a silent laugh.

"I know," Lynch said, still panting. "Saw them—the horses."

Debrett shook his head. "No—us. One white"—he waved at Lynch—"one black"—a tap on his own chest—"and now we're both khaki from the dust!"

Lynch made a gesture upward, and Debrett nodded. Slowly, searching out every handhold on the coach's trimming, moving with extreme care so as not to tip it and alert the unwary passenger—and, for the same reason, avoiding the oval window in the rear—they climbed to the top of the speeding vehicle.

Two red backs with crossed white belts confronted them. Good—the soldiers handling the driving had seen and felt nothing to alarm them. Ned and Nick wormed their bodies over the edge of the roof, and, knees flexed, balancing on the swaying surface—child's play to men accustomed to threading their way along the narrow, slick spars of a ship pitching in a gale—moved to crouch behind the soldiers. In unison, their hands reached forward . . .

Major Folly's absorption in the densely printed page of General Sir Ralph Hounslow's book on naval warfare was so complete that he did not notice the sudden appearance and equally sudden disappearance of one of the soldiers driving him at the left-side window of the coach. Nor did the fall of the man on the right attract his attention.

But after a moment, something did draw his concentration from *Soldiers at Sea,* in spite of Sir Ralph's ingenious explanation of how the Battle of Agincourt would have come out differently if it had been fought at sea rather than on land. The coach was slowing. And it was moving far more quietly and smoothly than it should have on the rutted surface of the highway. And it was passing landmarks totally unfamiliar to Major Folly. And now it had stopped completely. In short, it was not where it was supposed to be at all—in fact, as a gleam of water through the window showed him, it was at the edge of a beach cove!

In a rage, mingled with a sudden, unreasoning apprehension, Major Folly reached for the door handle on the left side of the coach—then drew back as Ned Lynch's inverted, grinning face appeared in the window.

He snatched at the other door, and again withdrew from it at the sight of Nick Debrett's face, also upside down, blocking that window. The white eye patch, in that position, was an extra touch of grotesquery that made him feel slightly ill.

Both doors opened, and the two pirates swung into the coach easily, taking the outer places on the narrow seat and wedging Folly between them. They were covered with dust and reeking with sweat, giving Folly the feeling that he was being squeezed between two giant, deadly beasts of prey. He made a grab at his sword hilt, but could not get a purchase on it in the crush.

Lynch leaned over and looked at the book still open in Folly's lap. "Ah, old Houndstooth's hobbyhorse, and himself at sea even when he was on land. Actually, Major Folly, it's *not* a very good book. I would suggest the work done by Mollet and Van der Veer on the same subject. *Far* more comprehensive," he drawled.

Folly gritted his teeth, his outrage overcoming his fear for the moment. "I swore to you before, and I will swear to you again, Captain Lynch—*I will see you hang!*"

Lynch and Debrett exchanged glances across Folly's head. Lynch said sorrowfully, "I think the major takes this amiss, Nick."

Debrett shook his head in mock regret. "So it seems, Captain. And what a shame! Now I'm beginning to doubt he'd even accept *my* apology."

"Which one would that be, now?" Lynch inquired, leaning across Folly in such a way as to squeeze an involuntary grunt out of him.

"Why, for leaving my lodging in such a hurry that I never had the time to thank him for his hospitality." Debrett also was now lounging on Folly, and both pirates' heads were almost in front of his face. He had a mad desire to bite one of the ears flaunted in front of him, but immediately rejected the idea as distasteful—literally so—and dangerous.

Ned Lynch sighed gustily. "Well, all a man can do is try to live a clean and honorable life, be kind to animals and women, and treat his fellow man as he would hope to be treated himself. Do you follow me, then?"

Debrett nodded solemnly. "So be it."

He grabbed Major Folly around the waist, kicked open the coach door, and deposited him on the sand. Ned Lynch wrestled the heavy chest out of the coach and dropped it, then strode up to the major and plucked his sword from its scabbard.

Fuming, Folly watched as the pirate captain, flourishing the major's sword derisively, and the damned black felon he'd so nearly managed to hang, hoisted the chest he had been particularly ordered to guard and bring to Lord Durant, and trotted down the beach with it toward the long boat he now saw nosing the shore line.

"Out with ye, Polonski, and beach it!" he heard a burly man in the boat's crew call. "A little boundin' and pullin' may be just what ye need to loosen up yer innards!"

Folly could not understand why a pirate should want to have his inward parts looser than they normally were, and did not care. He looked on, nearly blind with rage, as a tousle-headed man leaped from the boat and pulled it up onto the sand, as Debrett and Lynch swung the chest into the longboat, and as Lynch turned and thrust his sword deep into the sand.

"Fare ye well, Major Folly," Lynch called from the water's edge. "And cheer up: there are brighter days ahead!"

He vaulted into the boat. Debrett, there already, muttered, "That was unkind, Ned. What sort of brighter days can that poor piece of English mutton expect?"

"Ah, now," Lynch said. "Wouldn't you say *any* day other than this one—when he has to tell My Lord Durant that this nice bit of treasure he was already seeing himself spending has gone off with the Gypsies, as you might say—would *have* to be brighter? Always providing he lives to see it, of course, which even a wagering man like myself wouldn't care to venture on. . . . All right, Polonski, push her off."

Polonski, digging his feet into the soft sand, gave a mighty thrust at the longboat. It moved backward . . . and so did he, his feet slipping, scrabbling, and failing to find purchase. The boat, free of the beach, drifted out; Polonski, like a living mooring rope, was stretched flat on his face in the water between boat and shore. The pirate oarsmen jeered and catcalled as Polonski began swimming toward them; Mr. Moonbeam gave a reproving roar and reached over the gunwales to help the floundering man aboard.

At the waterline, retrieving his sword from the sand, Folly looked bitterly after them. If one of the wretches had drowned, that would at least have been *something*. But if every man jack on the *Blarney Cock* were to die of the plague this very day, they would probably be happier than Charles Austin Lepied Folly: painfully dead though they might be, they would not have to look forward to explaining to Lord James Durant that he was not to have Sir James Barnet's treasure.

He sighed, slapped the clinging grains of sand from his sword and returned it to his scabbard, then trudged over to the horses, who had drawn the coach to the water's edge and were now staring with imbecile interest at the sea. The last the men in the longboat saw of him, he was hitting at them with the flat of his sword, trying to get them to move. He did not seem to be making any impression on them.

Ned Lynch patted the chest and observed sententiously, "A major's lot is not a happy one. Now, Nick, doesn't this make you feel rich, just having this grand chest, stuffed with money and jewels, on board?"

"I could feel richer," Debrett said quietly.

"How so?"

The black man shook his head mournfully. "Ah, he forgets so soon, when it comes to paying a wager. What I could feel richer by, Captain Lynch, sir, is six doubloons that I won from you in our race back yonder."

"Won!" Lynch burst out. "Why, you never . . . Wait, now, so you did, come to think of it. By a finger's breadth, no more, though." And, grumbling, he dipped into his pouch for the gold pieces. He looked up as he heard the oarsmen's laughter. Nick Debrett was demonstrating a "finger's breadth" to his amused audience by extending the middle digit of his right hand and clenching the others.

Lynch frowned, then burst out laughing himself. "By God, we'd do better to have that for a sign on our flag, Nick, than that moldy old skull and crossbones—for sure, it's the way we live in this world: give the finger or get it!"

Chapter 6

Sunset on the island of Jamaica can be a glorious finish to a superb day, smearing the western sky with a lavish palette of gold, rose, crimson, and the rare but prized flash of green just as the sun dips below the ocean horizon. For the best effect, a suitable vantage point is required, such as the Barnets' house in the hills; and Lady Barnet, for more than ten years, and Jane, for the few brief months she had been in Jamaica, had enjoyed the sight deeply.

But in the moldering, shabby streets of the oldest part of Kingston, the westering sun threw only a lurid, gloomy red on the peeling stucco walls, seeming to replace their patchy, fading paint with fresh blood. This near the horizon, it left the piles of refuse in the street in merciful shadow, but a stabbing ray now and then picked out one or another grotesque face or form among the hundreds of people swarming there, illuminating them for the dismayed Lady Barnet as she looked from her coach—hers for only another few moments, for after delivering her and her daughter to some dismal lodging nearby, it was to be taken to Lord Durant as part of Sir James Barnet's forfeited estate.

Nearly half of Lady Barnet's adult life had been spent in the house in the hills, with visits only to the best shops, receptions at the fortress, and dinners at the homes of Jamaica's officials and wealthy planters. The raw life of Kingston's back streets was a revelation, and a visceral shock, to her. Jane Barnet, on the other hand, dispatched to school in Paris at the age of nine, when her father had received his appointment to Jamaica—there was a firm tradition that English children exposed to the tropics would straightaway die of a fever, or, worse, mature too early and embrace exotic vices—had spent ten years in that ancient city, contriving to explore many of its less savory purlicus. To a girl who had seen something of what went on in the twisting streets off the Boulevard St.-Michel or behind the Louvre, the slums of Kingston looked comparatively modern and wholesome, though nonetheless depressing and dangerous for that. There was a difference between being a schoolgirl on an escapade and having to live in such a place.

The coach passed under a rope stretched taut across the street from one second-story window to another; on it, a figure in brightly patched clothes capered nimbly, always seeming on the point of plummeting to the pavement, but never doing so. A drunken soldier leaned out of a window farther down the street and shouted incoherent encouragement; another scaled a chamber pot at him, as though bowling at a tenpin. The tightrope walker caught it deftly and held it behind himself for a moment, then pantomimed emptying it into the street with a dainty gesture of disgust which brought a screech of laughter from the crowd. Coins—all copper—arced up from the street and from watchers at windows; he caught most of them in the chamber pot, and the others clattered to the street, where ragged beggars shoved and struck to get at them.

Jane peered out the window to catch the last of the curious spectacle, then lost sight of it as the coach turned down a narrow street that led to the waterfront. Another turn, and Mason—the Barnet family servant who had seen to their needs during their life on the island, and with whom Jane, in her few months there, had established a fond relationship, being the only person in the household able to approximate the French he had learned in his native Haiti—drew the horse to a halt.

Jane looked out at the cracked, weathered lodging

house fronting the Kingston docks that stood next to them. Next to its shabby entrance, an unsteady sailor fumbled in the bodice of a woman pressed against the wall, and slobbered on the patient, painted face above it, then broke away and lurched toward the longboat that waited to take him and his companions out to their ship in the harbor.

"We're here, Mother," she said flatly.

"Dear God!" Lady Barnet murmured. She shrank back as a distorted face appeared in the window of the door on her side, and a gnarled claw of a hand scrabbled on the glass. The beggars of Kingston were out in force, and now surrounded the coach, demanding with slurring whine and sly gesture whatever coins the passengers in this fashionable coach could spare.

Lady Barnet was sunk in misery and horror, and did not even note the sudden change that took place when a withered crone in the crowd began jabbing at the most persistent beggars with her cane. "That's Sir James's family," she hissed. "Leave them alone. They've problems enough tonight." She waved her stick toward the brooding silhouette of the fortress, humped like a sleeping elephant against the deepening purple of the sky. "Sir James is in *there* . . . and they're here amongst the likes of us. Let them be, do you hear?"

To Jane's interested surprise, the beggars seemed to molt away into the shadows. So . . . among the lost and disinherited of Kingston, the name of Sir James Barnet still meant something—enough, at least, to call for some forbearance toward his family. It could be important to remember that. . . .

It was clear that the Barnet name also meant something to the landlady of the mean lodging house they now entered. She seemed to take a venomous delight at showing these fine ladies the squalor of the room allotted to them, and to savor the few sticks of splintery furniture, the cracked and peeling walls, and the ugly bed with its torn mattress; to Jane, she seemed to be a blood relative to the fat rat that glared at them defiantly from the center of the floor before scuttling into the darkness.

"It does not please milady?" The woman's voice was mocking.

"Leave us alone," Lady Barnet said bleakly.

"Indeed I will, madam—*after* I have been paid." The landlady gave a muted titter, as if enjoying the finest of jokes—and, to be sure, after a street accident or a drunkard's fall from a high window, what could be more amusing than the spectacle of two pampered women who had last night slept on fine linen in a great mansion being suddenly thrust into this place, and into her power?

Lady Barnet took three coins from her purse and handed them to the woman, saying grimly, "It is far too much for a rathole like this."

Jane's lips tightened. Mother was quite right, of course, but she was in a new world now, with new rules, and plain speaking was a luxury, perhaps an expensive one, not a right. Jane hated her surroundings as much as her mother did, but had already accepted the need to find a way to adapt to them—if possible, to use them.

The landlady almost spat as she spoke. "Watch your tongue . . . my lady. This is my home."

"Then," Lady Barnet said, making an effort to stay in control of her voice, which threatened to quaver, "we are as sorry for you as we are for the fate that brought us to it."

"Needn't waste your *pity* on me, madam," the landlady said, bridling. "Unlike you, I am where I choose to be."

She slammed the door as she left the room, and the single candle on the rough table flickered for a moment. Lady Barnet's fingers clenched and loosened, as though she had been reaching for something heavy to throw at her.

Mason, who had impassively accompanied Jane and her mother into their lodgings, set down the valises he had carried from the coach. He turned to Lady Barnet, then to Jane. "It grieves me, my ladies. It surely grieves me." His voice broke, and he was unable to continue.

Jane reached for his hand with both of hers and clasped it. *"A bientôt, mon brave Mason,"* she murmured. *"A la fin, on les aura, hein?"*

Even in this moment of supreme sadness, a flicker of respectful amusement passed across Mason's face at Jane's deliberate use of Paris slum argot, delivered in a street urchin's growl . . . and, could be she was right, at the end, and *they* would get what was coming to them. . . . He looked at the proud young face, and realized with pride and grief that it had aged and hardened in the last few hours. Mademoiselle Jane was growing up—and it would not be well with those who had made her do so. He quickly bent and kissed her hand, then turned to Lady Barnet.

"When we are recovered, we will send for you, Mason. You have my word on that."

Her voice was firm, but it carried no conviction. Lady Barnet had not always been the easiest of mistresses, but she had been fair and had known how to use power with an aristocrat's ease; it nearly broke Mason's heart to see her helpless and broken like this. He nodded, turned away, and left the room, keeping back the tears that shamed him until he was in the darkened hallway.

Lady Barnet sank weakly into one of the room's two chairs, unmindful of the stabbing of its cracked rush seating. Looking blindly at the flaking wall, she fumbled in the valise beside her and brought up a gold-backed hairbrush. She held it up so that the light from the candle fell on its handle, and her lips moved as she read, whispering to herself, the inscription engraved on it: *To my bride, with all my love. James.*

It was the only object of value that they had risked defying Lord Durant's edict by removing from the house. When Lady Barnet had insisted on taking it, Jane had been impatient, pointing out the danger they courted; now, she was glad that her mother had it—she would need something tangible of her former life to hold onto if she were to have any hope of staying a whole person.

In sending their daughter to Paris for her education, the Barnets had got, though they were unaware of it, more than they had bargained for. The school, though a strict one, had had low walls, and Jane had always been a venturesome child. Though not directly affected, at least to the extent of participating in it, by the seamier side of life in the Sun King's capital, she had learned a great deal more of life—and language—than her parents had any idea of. And it seemed to her that that was all to the good. Something would have to be done, and there was only Jane herself to do it.

She pushed open the creaking shutters and leaned on the windowsill. The raucous sounds of the neighborhood and the pungent smells of the street, overlaid with the salt tang of the harbor, flooded into the room like an alien invasion. Jane looked past the sea of rooftops and chimneys to the brooding bulk of the fortress.

Her right hand slid inside a fold of her dress and clenched on the handle of her dagger as she spoke, saying the words aloud to emphasize their solemnity. "He will be free. And Durant will pay. *This I promise.*"

The sunset that had illuminated in so sinister a manner the Barnet women's new neighborhood had passed almost unnoticed aboard the *Blarney Cock*. The ship's decks were almost as crowded and noisy as the streets of Kingston at dusk, though the throng was less varied. There were, in fact, only two categories of people: pirates and whores. Anticipating the wealth that would accrue to the ship when Mr. Moonbeam and Polonski finally succeeded in opening the chest he and Debrett had snatched from Major Folly, Ned Lynch had sent two longboats from the sheltered cove to Kingston, with their crews ordered to bring back casks of the best wine, baskets of the best food, and a dozen or so of the most versatile and enthusiastic girls that the town could offer. What was the use of piracy if you couldn't treat yourself to a little celebration now and then? was the way Lynch saw it.

Nick Debrett stood with each arm around a girl; a third, in front of him, pressed against him without needing to be held. It was hard to tell whether Nick and the girls were more aroused by each other or by the chest now being vigorously attacked with a steel pry bar by Polonski and Mr. Moonbeam. Debrett thought that it was probably about equal, and anyhow, mixed together; the lust for riches and the fevers of the body fed and enhanced each other, and he knew for a fact that when he had money to burn, the women looked better, felt better, and came his way a lot easier. He let his fingers explore the girls on either side, and at the same time moved gently but authoritatively against the body of the one leaning on him. All four of them looked avidly at the still-unopened chest.

An expression of hope spread on Polonski's face, and he rose. Debrett and the girls leaned forward: had the lock finally given way? But Polonski laid down the bar and hurried toward the prow, tugging at the sash around his waist. "Good luck, friend!" Mr. Moonbeam called after him.

"What's that about?" one of the girls said. "Did he decide he had something better to do than opening a treasure chest?"

Debrett grinned and explained Polonski's problem. The girl was sympathetic. "Ten days—that's bad. Has he tried figs? Figs is wonderful that way."

"'Tisn't figs you want, then, it's coconut milk," the girl on Debrett's left arm said wisely. "It's the oil in it does it, you see, works around in there and loosens you proper, has you clean as a whistle in no time."

"It tastes awful, but I'd swear by soapy water," the third girl chimed in. "I was that way once, and by accident, like, swallowed some wash water, and in not above five minutes . . ."

Debrett suddenly found that his interest was more on the chest than on the women, detached himself from them, and strode forward to lend Mr. Moonbeam a hand.

He leaned on the end of the pry bar, and the heavy lock finally yielded and tore away from the chest. Ned Lynch, with a sultry, buxom beauty in tow, moved up to the chest as Debrett and Mr. Moonbeam threw back the lid and disclosed a brilliant array of jewels and valuables: rubies and emeralds winked red and green in the flickering torchlight that lit the deck, and the gleam of gold was everywhere.

The crew was ecstatic. "Hey, now, that's some-thing like!" "More there than on many a merchantman, I'll be bound!" "Ah, Red Ned, you're a good provider for yer poor family!" A few merely whooped and began dipping into the treasure, bringing up handfuls of gold pieces, necklaces, pendants, and other ornaments. Others pounded Lynch and Debrett on the back in a delirium of appreciation.

One of Nick Debrett's girls discovered a long neck-lace of perfectly matched pearls and draped it around her neck, admiring its pale splendor against her dusky skin. It hung on her breasts like a chain of snowflakes, its lower end disappearing between them into her loos-ened bodice.

"Not that, my angel," Debrett said gently.

The girl pouted. "But I like it, Nick!"

He deftly withdrew it, disarranging the bodice further, returned it to the chest, and rummaged for a moment before straightening up. "Here, now, that's what you'll want." He handed her a pair of exquisitely carved marble elephants, flat at facing sides and bot-tom, fashioned to serve as bookends.

The girl hefted them uncertainly. "But what am I to do with these?"

"Fill the space between with books, my sweet, rath-er than your body with jewels," Debrett said solemnly. "What good is it to have a decorated neck when an empty head is perched on top?"

There was a general roar of laughter from the crewmen nearby, and Mr. Moonbeam called out, "Are these young ladies your pupils, then, Nick, and you the schoolmaster? I'll warrant you set them some good les-sons—and aren't sparing with the rod when it comes to that, if you take my meaning!"

Ned Lynch reached into the chest and retrieved the pearl necklace. He tossed it to his own girl and grinned at Nick Debrett. "Better an empty head than an empty bed!"

As the crew's laughter broke out again, Debrett winked at Lynch, grabbed his three girls, and shepherded them toward a hatch that led below decks.

Lynch's girl ferreted among the jewels on her own, and now held up a magnificent ruby brooch, a giant stone set in intricate, delicate gold filigree. She showed it to Lynch with an imploring glance. When he nodded in agreement, she leaped to her feet and embraced him with an enthusiasm that threatened the stability of her low-cut dress.

As the crew cheered, Ned called out to them, "Division of the spoils at eight bells. Any man caught thieving is keel-hauled. Mr. Polonski!"

The crew grew quiet, and Ned looked around, not seeing the Polish seaman any place among them. He did notice that there was an air of subdued hilarity about some of them, as if they knew something he did not.

"Where'd he go?" After a pause, some of the crew moved aside, opening a gap through which Ned could see forward to where Polonski perched like a forlorn seagull over the beakhead grating.

"Still?" Ned said in surprise.

"Ten days now, Cap'n," Mr. Moonbeam said mournfully.

Lynch shook his head in sympathy. "That's a long time to be without relief."

"Ten days is a long time to be without anything!" his girl said, and broke into a hoot of helpless laughter, which spread to the crew. In a moment, all were roaring; the distant figure of Polonski seemed to quiver and shrink a little as the sound came to him.

Lynch bent, took the girl behind the knees, and straightened, slinging her over his shoulder as easily as if she had been a roll of carpeting, an act which burst the last restraining neckline buttons and left her in effect naked to the waist. The crew cheered the sight, and the girl, unabashed, waved jauntily at them, setting up a pleasing quiver that roused them to further enthusiasm.

"Mr. Moonbeam!"

"Aye, aye, sir!"

He pointed to the chest. "I'm holding you responsible."

"Aye, aye, Cap'n." Mr. Moonbeam slammed the lid on the chest and sat on it, with a musket laid out next to one hand and a cutlass by the other.

"Good night, lads!" Lynch called out, making for the hatch. "Sleep well!" As he disappeared down the hatchway, the roistering crew had a last look at the girl on his shoulder. Ecstatic over the jewels she had been given, and the other delights she was about to receive, she was blowing kisses to them.

Hours later, the *Blarney Cock* was quiet, or nearly so. The revelry had died away as the last of the seamen, having exhausted their capacities for food, drink, and women, slumbered, some in their hammocks, some on the floor below them; some alone, some companioned. The ship rocked gently at anchor, soothing and deepening the sleep of even the land-accustomed Kingston girls.

Chapter 7

The vast room, being set up for Lord Durant's comfort alone, seemed like a steam bath to Major Folly, sweating in his full uniform. Though, near midnight, Jamaica was normally pleasantly cool, the air in the huge bathroom was nearly at blood temperature, and the flaring torches in sconces on the wall added steadily to the heat.

Folly was beginning to feel that he had made a mistake in accepting Lord Durant's takeover of authority. True, those who opposed him were harshly dealt with; but the situation of Sir James Barnet, with nothing more to worry him than the prospect of rotting for months in a filthy cell, struck the major as positively enviable.

He glanced nervously around the shadowed room. The strange girls in their varied costumes, motionless and expressionless; the positively unnerving lute player, drawing the sweetest of music from his instrument while his gaze was fixed on something Folly could not see—and perhaps no living man could; the dark woman, as ripely sensual as the highest-priced trull in Kingston, yet somehow completely unavailable, at least to a normal man; the impassive, huge black standing behind Folly, and the other, equally outsized, bending over Durant—all these uncanny members of Durant's entourage contributed to his steadily growing feeling of unease.

The major source of that feeling was, of course,

Lord Durant. Now stretched out naked, face down on a cushioned table, he presented a sight that both sickened and frightened Folly. He could not bear to look at the man—yet it was this pink, flabby creature who had the power of life and death over him, as over so many on the island.

Durant's attendant dipped a giant hand into a pot of melted wax that simmered over a brazier on the floor, and gently coated his master's back with it. Once the entire surface was covered thickly, he fanned it to dryness with slow waves of a palm frond.

The smell of the wax, and the corpselike appearance of Durant's back as it cooled, were making Folly feel more upset than ever. So far, his account of what had happened to Sir James Barnet's treasure chest had caused none of Durant's usual venomous tirades, but the major knew better than to hope that that state of things would last. Durant was at his most dangerous when most quiet.

He gulped, then forced himself to speak. "I plead with you, Lord Durant, to give me one last chance, one final opportunity to redeem myself in your noble eyes. As God is my witness, I shall not fail you again." He hoped he had got across the proper fawning, cringing tone that Durant favored in those who spoke to him—and for once, the fawning and cringing came from the bottom of his heart.

Durant nodded slowly; it was almost as if he were moving his head in order to enjoy the texture of the velvet pillow beneath his face rather than making any gesture in reply to Folly's plea. Now the wax on his back was whitening even more as it hardened; the torchlight flickered in the dark's woman's eyes, lending a momentary semblance of expression to her still face. Folly waited for Durant to speak, desperate for him to do so and thus end the suspense, yet fearing the moment.

"Dear, dear Major Folly. *Young* Major Folly . . . so *very* young." Durant's voice was muffled by the pillow, and Folly was both outraged that the man could not be bothered to face him as he spoke and grateful that he was not turning his deceptively mild gaze Folly's way. "What ever am I to do with you? First, the one-eyed prisoner . . . then my own personal treasure, *entrusted* to you . . ."

He shook his head as if in profound distress and disappointment, and sighed weightily. Folly lowered his eyes. Whatever it was, it was going to be bad—and it was coming soon.

"But . . . never let it be said that Lord Durant is not a fair man." Folly looked up, startled, and beginning to allow himself a gleam of hope.

"So be it, my earnest major," Durant said heartily, finally turning his face toward Folly and displaying a gently forgiving smile. "So be it. One last chance you indeed shall have."

Folly, nearly dazed with relief and delight, looked at Durant with new eyes. After all, no harm in a man taking care of himself, and indulging himself as he liked in his own home . . . and doubtless, when you got to know them, the dark woman, the odd fellow with the lute, and those dress-up wenches along the wall were cheerful enough company. It didn't do to misjudge . . .

"However." Always a word marking a reversal, this one was spoken in a tone of gloating amusement that extinguished Folly's hopes in a moment and seemed to send his heart plummeting to his boots. "Like the child who must be spanked in order that he may better remember his lesson, so must it be sometimes with men . . . like you, dear Major."

Folly tensed. Without having to turn around, he was vividly aware of the giant black servant behind him, and could remember all too clearly the man's monstrously developed arm and chest muscles. He could picture the thrashing he would receive, and could only hope that his fellow officers and his men would never get to hear of it. Well, humiliation and some bruises were not the worst thing that could happen to a man. . . .

Lord Durant turned his gaze toward where the dreamy, youthful lute player sat on a cushion and strummed. He gave a slight smile, reflected by a momentary flicker from the youth's pale face. "Take off your coat, Major Folly," Durant said softly.

"Beg pardon, sir?"

"And your shirt as well."

Folly, desperately trying to make himself believe that this order to strip to the waist was no more than standard preparation for a beating, found himself unable to move. The lute player laid down his instrument and rose in a single slow, graceful movement from his cushion. Folly's fingers plucked at a coat button and dropped away again. It seemed to him that he was slowly dissolving inside.

Seeing the major helpless to follow instructions, Durant gave a curt nod to the servant standing behind the officer. The giant hands reached around, grasped Folly's uniform collar, and pulled. Brass buttons popped loose as easily as peas from a pod and rolled on the floor, winking mockingly at Folly as they caught the glimmer of torchlight; his arms seemed as if they were about to be wrenched from their sockets; then the coat was off. He was gasping with pain, outrage, and shock, but made no move to resist as his shirt was ripped from him; then, almost in the same movement, the massive servant caught him under the arms, dragged him a few paces across the floor, and flung him backward onto a chaise longue.

Folly stared wildly at the lute player, who now stood over him. Beyond, he could see the dark woman seated at the edge of the empty marble bath; with unreasoning horror he noted that one hand was stroking her nearly exposed breast, slowly, lovingly.

The horror began to become sharp and specific as he watched the lute player reach into a tunic pocket and withdraw a leather case. From it he took a shimmering length of steel, at least three inches long, filed at one end to a needle-sharp tip, at the other displaying a small circular clamp the size of a finger ring. The youth, still wearing his faraway look, slid it onto the index finger of his right hand; the tip protruded more than an inch beyond the fingertip. Major Folly's tongue scraped over bone-dry lips; he found he could not help watching as a second claw was attached, and a third . . .

Though it was an effort to turn his head to the proper angle, Durant observed the slow, graceful movements of the one young man and the passive terror of the other with loving interest. The dark woman looked at him steadily.

He murmured to her, "The words of my dear friend Alexander Pope leap into my mind:

" 'Vice is a monster of so frightful mien
As to be hated needs but to be seen.
Yet seen too oft, familiar with her face,
We first endure, then pity, then embrace.' "

The dark woman merely looked at him with the same unchanging intensity.

Both the lute player's hands were now fully clawed, shimmering in the torchlight, and rested lightly on the major's bare chest. The chill of the cold steel made him gasp involuntarily.

Durant nodded to the lute player, and the steel claws began to dance on Folly's skin, as if plucking a melody from his instrument—and indeed, the whimpering that Folly could not suppress at the first stabbing pains was as sweet in Lord Durant's ears as any music.

"Suffering," he said to his companion, "becomes all mankind, but it finds its most perfect expression in the faces of the young."

The dark woman did not reply. Durant extended a hand in a gesture of gentle command, and she gave a barely perceptible nod toward one of the scantily clad girls against the wall. Moving slowly and cautiously, the one thus summoned approached Durant, and, long practiced in the routine, ran a finger lightly over his back, outlining the area covered by the wax.

By now the lute player's fingers were dancing faster than the eye could follow, and Major Folly's hoarse, hopeless cries rang through the room. Durant stirred sluggishly on the cushioned table; the dark woman eyed him and gave another nod. The girl standing over Durant knelt beside him, leaning forward so that her nearly bared bosom was within inches of his face. Another gesture from the dark woman brought a second girl forward to take up the same position on the other side of the table.

There was a practiced quality to these movements, to every aspect of the sequence of events in the room, as if everything that had happened and was to happen next had been repeated many, many times—for the very good reason that it had been so repeated. . . .

Durant, the impassive black servant above him, and the three women near him seemed to be waiting for the next stage in the unfolding ritual, and a slight but detectable tension infused their movements and stances as it came with an inhuman, bubbling scream from Major Folly.

Durant spoke thickly. "Dagon. Time enough. Remove the wax."

The black man set aside his palm frond and gently reached for the edges of the layer of dried wax on his master's back. Durant stared deeply into the dark woman's eyes and squeezed the hands of the girls on either side of him, bracing himself for the short but sharp pain which was to come.

"Now!"

Dagon wrenched the adhesivelike layer of congealed wax from Lord Durant's skin, bringing with it most of the mat of hair that had covered his back. Durant twitched and let out a brief moan that might have been of pleasure or pain; the two girls' faces tensed with the effort not to show their own anguish as his grip tightened on their hands.

The black man held up the oblong of wax, which somewhat resembled the flayed hide of a sparsely furred animal, and studied it with satisfaction. He set it down and held a mirror so that Lord Durant could, with not too much effort, inspect the newly hairless portion of his back. Durant smiled at the sight of the smooth, rosy area, clean and soft as a baby's skin, then leaned to his left and let his lips graze on the breasts of the woman who knelt there.

The lute player's fingers now moved faster than ever, and Folly's screams blended into a continuous howl. Lord Durant turned to the woman on his right and buried his face in her bosom—never taking his eyes from those of the dark woman.

In the chill hour before the dawn, Folly's corporal was awakened by a soft but firm knock at the door of his quarters. He opened it cautiously, prepared to be severe with a soldier returning late. Outside, he saw a huge black man supporting, nearly carrying, an unconscious officer in a torn uniform. Through the rents in coat and shirt, it could be seen that a massive bandage covered his chest.

"Your major," the black said.

"What's . . . what's happened to him?" the corporal quavered. "Looks like he fell into a bear pit or some such."

"Visit to Lord Durant." The black gave a mirthless grin. "For interview. You want to know more?"

"No . . . n-n-no," the corporal said. "That's quite all right, no business of mine, I'm sure, my good man." He accepted the burden of the sagging major, staggering under the weight. "Um . . . obliged to you for helping the major here, very kind of you."

The black looked down at the officer whose flesh he had watched being sliced by the flashing steel claws, remembering the screams, the writhing, and the smell of fresh blood.

"My pleasure," he said.

Chapter 8

Some landlocked nations have been able to attain a kind of freedom, but the general rule has always been that the more seacoast a land has, the less its people can be controlled. Men willing to hazard their lives for whatever the sea can bring them in the way of fish, trade, or plunder are not amenable subjects to any authority; and even the shore-based people who deal with such men catch something of the infection of their independence, and share their view of government as an understood adversary. Thus it was that Ned Lynch and picked members of his crew—including Nick Debrett, Mr. Moonbeam, and Polonski—together with some of their female companions of the previous night, felt secure in coming ashore openly on Kingston's waterfront shortly before noon.

Ned had chosen their landing prudently, of course: a wharf favored by the middling tradesmen who profited most from the buccaneers' trade, rather than where the aristocracy's and officials' skiffs and barges were moored, or where the shabby craft of those sinking to ultimate poverty lay—duty might drive the frequenters of one location, and fear and grinding need those of the other, to advise Lord Durant of the presence of the pirate captain who had flouted him twice within little more than a day.

Lynch handed his girl ashore, making sure that her feet were set firmly on the slimy stone steps that led up to street level, then stepped lightly from the longboat; the others followed, prepared for a glorious exploration of Kingston's fleshpots.

The warmth of the air, the cries of the marketplace vendors and entertainers, the sights and varied odors of Kingston surrounded and cheered the whole party. At a fruit seller's stall Ned snatched three papayas from a pile and juggled them; the fruit spun faster and faster in a blurred circle above his darting hands. The girl who had shared his bunk—the coarse sailor's thread which held her buttonless bodice together contrasting strangely with the gleam of the ruby-and-gold brooch from Sir James Barnet's treasure chest pinned to her neckline—laughed in delight, her lips still swollen and slack from her spirited joustings of the night before.

The papayas spun yet faster in front of Ned Lynch's face; then the one nearest his nose, in its downward circuit, suddenly divided itself into two unbalanced halves that tumbled past his swiftly moving hands and smashed onto the pavement. It seemed as if the spinning fruit had been split by a steely flicker of light, but the dagger quivering in the wall behind Lynch's head showed the true cause.

In an instant, Ned Lynch's cutlass was out of its sheath and weaving defensively in front of him as he fell into a swordsman's crouch. A pistol appeared in Mr. Moonbeam's hand, and Polonski armed himself by wrenching two spokes from the wheel of a vegetable cart and holding them in an X, buttressed at their intersection by his crossed wrists—the classic position of the Krakow quarterstaff fighter; he ignored the yells of the cart's owner as it collapsed, spewing its contents into the street.

Ned Lynch's eyes darted around the crowded marketplace. There was no visible enemy, yet the dagger still remained in the wall as evidence of a near-lethal assault.

Could it be one of his crew, thinking to make a space at the top? Or a toady of Durant's? Maybe a woman he'd outraged . . . by not outraging her enough? And what the devil was Nick Debrett laughing at, like some black loon? Lynch cast a malign glance at his illtimedly mirthful mate, then followed the direction of Nick's pointing finger.

Another black man, younger and looser than Debrett, though as tall and broadly built, stepped from the shadows behind a market stall, smiling widely and moving with the lithe ease of a dancer. Ned Lynch's eyes narrowed as he saw the leather bandolierlike harness that angled across the man's chest; it had a dozen sheaths stitched into its surface, eleven of which were filled with daggers identical to the one that had just whizzed past his nose.

"Cudjo!" Debrett called out delightedly.

"At yo' sarvice, sir," the man rumbled. Unlike the widely traveled Debrett, his voice still held the rich lilt of island speech.

"I take it," Ned Lynch said stiffly, "this man's a friend of yours?" That dagger had come too close for him to feel entirely amiable toward the new arrival just yet.

"Friend?" Debrett said joyously. "No . . . more than that!" He embraced the man called Cudjo and was himself hugged in turn; with an effort, he lifted him from the ground, and found himself lifted exuberantly.

"So . . . where have you been, my very large friend?"

"I have been *abroad,* little Nick! Abroad! Island-hopping! Following the wind, free like a bird, and pinching a plump behind wherever I can find one!" He laughed, a cascade of pure delight. "And you, little Nick . . . the *tales* I am told, man! A scoundrel, that Nick Debrett! A bri*gand!*"

Debrett grinned, looking younger and more carefree than Ned Lynch ever remembered seeing him. "All true, my friend. And much, much worse!"

Cudjo looked inquiringly at Lynch. "And this gentleman, whose nose I came so close to removing?"

Debrett drew them together. "Ned Lynch . . . Cudjo Quarrel."

"It is an honor, Captain Lynch," Quarrel said, shaking his hand enthusiastically.

"And how do you come to know *my* friend?"

Lynch asked. This Cudjo Quarrel was something unexpected; in the seven years he had sailed with Nick Debrett, he had learned almost nothing of his past, and absolutely nothing about any old friends from his prepiracy life.

"Little Nick and I shared many a length of *chain"*—Quarrel drew the last word out with mocking emphasis—"and when the day came that we finally grew tired of one another's company, there was only one thing for us to do. . . ." He made a sudden sharp gesture, pantomiming the breaking of a chain with bare hands; Lynch more than half-suspected that it also stood for breaking the neck of a slave overseer or so. "We blew our separate ways, as free men will, Nick to the *Blarney Cock,* as I hear it, and me wherever I found a pleasing breeze."

He plucked his dagger from the wall beside Lynch, and returned it to the empty pouch on his chest. Debrett clapped him on the shoulder.

"It's good to be on the same tack again, Cudjo."

"Breezes tend to blow that way, old friend."

Now that the dagger had been linked with an owner, and put safely away, Lynch felt a bit more relaxed. "A pleasure to meet my friend Nick's friend."

"A treat for me too, Captain."

Fully prepared to accept Cudjo, Lynch said, "We're on a course for the Bull's Foot for some drink. Will you not join us?"

Quarrel shook his head. "Another time, for certain. Kingston's not so large that Nick and I won't find each other again."

After a final embrace from Debrett, the pirates and their attendant women made off down the crowded street.

Polonski, grateful for the use of the vegetable vendor's wheel spokes, returned them and clapped the man on the back to express his thanks, inadvertently sending him sprawling in the street. Mr. Moonbeam put an armlock on Polonski and dragged him off, pausing for a moment to turn and heave a gold doubloon in the direction of the ruined wagon and its proprietor.

"This'll fix yer cart, then," he called back, "and get you a new load of truck to sell from it. I'll not have you saying that poor men suffered when Ned Lynch's men passed by."

As he hurried with Polonski to catch up with the others, Mr. Moonbeam made a mental note to dun the captain for the expenditure of the doubloon—after all, it had been spent in the cause of keeping up the *Blarney Cock*'s reputation, so should be a ship's expense, not his.

Twenty paces away, a man, better dressed than most in the crowd, lurked behind a wandering sightseer. His fingers hovered over the man's bulging coat pocket, then jerked spasmodically as his sleeve was pinned to the edge of a market stall by a knife that seemed suddenly to have grown there.

The pickpocket's intended victim passed on, unaware and, in fact, made notably uneasy by the exploding burst of laughter from the huge black man with that strange garment or pouch or whatever it was strung across his chest. Farther down the twisting street, the party from the *Blarney Cock* made for the sign in the shape of a huge hoof projecting over the pavement. As they turned in to the tavern entrance, Ned Lynch was briefly aware of an unusually well-dressed, unusually pretty brunette girl staring at them with unusual intensity. His practiced eye noted and assessed her youthful desirability; he filed the judgment away for future action—if the girl were from this neighborhood, she'd be available, that was for sure.

Ten minutes or so earlier, Jane Barnet had learned firsthand of the general assumption that any woman encountered in this quarter was fair—and willing—game. Leaving her mother sunk in quiet apathy, she had left the lodging house to get some food. As she stepped onto the street, the glare of the sun hit her like a blow and dazzled her eyes, and a large hand grabbed her bottom, squeezing hard through the layers of linen dress and petticoat.

"Fancy wrappings," a slurred voice said. "Now, girl, what's the goods inside like?"

Jane blinked and saw an obviously drunken sailor standing over her, leering amiably. Before she could move away from the hand reaching behind her, his other was fumbling down the front of her dress. "Fresh and ripe, not as long on the vine as most of 'em," the sailor said. "And spirited, too, good for a nice, lively romp," he added, taking Jane's sudden desperate struggle to escape his encircling arm as evidence of enthusiasm for his offer.

He grinned foolishly at the laughter and jeers of the crowd, most of whom knew Jane's identity, for word of the Barnet women's enforced residence in their slum had spread rapidly. "Right you are, love," the sailor said. "Name your price, any price. Me ship sails within the hour, and I haven't a moment to lose—*Ow!*"

Jane had managed to free one knee, and now brought it up sharply. The sailor let her go, all interest in women suddenly displaced by a stabbing pain in his groin, and reeled back against a wall, clutching himself.

He stared reproachfully at Jane, who was twisting her disordered dress into place. "What'd you do that for? Did I say the wrong thing? Did I? Well, did I?"

Jane glared at him and pushed through the crowd.

"Wrong thing to the wrong woman, man," a street barber advised him. "That was none of your tearsheets, that was a lady."

"Lady!" the sailor said bitterly. "Fine kind o' lady, to be doin' that to a man—she's maybe unmanned me for life. Not even a whore'd do that."

The barber laughed. " 'Course not, man—that'd be killin' the goose as lays the golden eggs!"

Jane walked swiftly along the thronged street, collecting her thoughts. She realized she would have to keep moving. If she were to stop, she would once more be assumed to be offering herself for sale, or, more accurately, brief rental. She shuddered as she realized that her mother's money was almost gone, and there was no source of any more. It might be that, to keep alive, she would actually have to go on the streets, like most of the rest of the women here.

She studied the obvious whores as she passed them, and wondered what they were like, how they felt about what they did. Probably, she thought bitterly, they either didn't care, or they enjoyed it. . . . That one, now, just going into the tavern with that rough-looking crowd, most of the top of her squeezing out of her dress, as though she were offering a pair of melons for sale—she'd doubtless be happy in her work! And it seemed to pay well, from the glint of ruby and gold that flashed from her neckline. . . .

Jane stopped, oblivious of the jostling crowd, and stared hard. *That was her brooch!* Her most prized possession, sent to her in Paris on her sixteenth birthday, it had always enraptured her with its delicate tracery of gold and the rich red fire of its jewel; she could never be mistaken about it, even at this distance. She had last seen it yesterday morning, as her father's chest was closed and locked for the last time, awaiting removal by the soldiers acting under Durant's orders. How had it come here? No matter—it *was* here, and, by God, she would have it back!

She pushed into the tavern in time to hear the customers set up a roar. "It's Ned Lynch!" "Red Ned!" "Hey, Nick . . . Nick Debrett!" Drinkers set down their mugs and tankards and rushed to greet the pirates as old friends; the woman who had called to Debrett twined herself around him and gave him a long, deep kiss.

Jane stood near the door, trying to assess the situation. The doxy with the brooch was in the company of the man hailed as Red Ned. That would be the famous pirate, then, stories of whose exploits enlivened most Kingston dinner tables; Jane remembered her father fuming at the government's inability to bring him to book, but at the same time showing some admiration for his enterprise. "After all, he plunders as many enemy ships as English, so there is some public good that comes from his lawlessness," Sir James had once said. She studied him with interest and distaste—a well-enough set-up man, with a tigerish vigor about him, to be sure; yet, clearly crude and lecherous, and—the main point—buying his wench's soiled favors with Jane's brooch!

Her eyes fiercely on Lynch and his party, now seated at a table and calling on the landlord for drink, she paid no attention to the drunken soldier who appeared on the landing of the upper floor, and, buttoning his breeches, began lurching down the stairway. Halfway down, he swayed and caught at the rail to keep from falling. Out of the gabble of the drinkers, he caught a few words that seemed to sober him up instantly.

"That's Ned Lynch! The cheek of the man! Every court in the Indies has vowed to see him swing."

The man addressed muttered, "A man who steals from Durant can't be all that bad."

The soldier glanced around the tavern and saw that nearly all eyes were on the roistering party at the center table. Making himself as unobtrusive as possible, he slipped out of the building.

Jane tried to nerve herself for what she had to do. A proper lady would turn about and seek help, and, if none were forthcoming, resort to complaint and strategic fainting. But she was no longer a lady, not with her mother and herself consigned to a slum and her father in jail—and, she admitted, she had never had the makings of a proper lady, anyhow; there was too much independence and taste for direct action in her for that.

"Why do they call him *Red* Ned?" an owlish drinker near her asked a companion. "He's not a redhead."

"Because of the blood on his decks," his friend said with relish.

"Nay," another man corrected. "Because of the blood in his eye!"

Jane's lips tightened. Blood in his eye, indeed! In a moment or so, Master Lynch might be turning red from blood on his face! She pushed through the crowd, threading past the tables, ignoring the prods, squeezes, and offers that followed her, and made her way to Lynch's table.

Ned Lynch, recognizing the well-dressed girl who had stared at them so strangely outside the tavern, looked up. Jane stood over the unaware girl sporting her brooch, looked down fiercely for an instant, then grabbed a handful of her luxuriant hair and yanked violently. As the girl arched backward and screamed, Jane's free hand darted down, ripping the brooch away and leaving a large rent in the dress.

Jane tugged mercilessly at the girl's hair and said, "Where did you get this?"

The tavern crowd, noisy a moment before, now fell quiet. Ned and Nick Debrett, with no idea of what this bizarre attack meant, were fascinated and amused.

The girl wrenched against Jane's implacable grip. "Let go o' me!"

"Tell me! Where did you get this?" Jane darted the brooch at the girl's eyes; her victim screamed theatrically, seeming to hope to prod her protector into action.

"I gave it to her," Ned Lynch said coolly.

Jane relaxed her grip on the girl's hair, and the screaming subsided to an aggrieved string of muttered curses.

Jane faced Lynch. "Where did you get it?"

Ned Lynch glanced at Debrett and smiled. "Where did *I* get it, you say?"

The thought of anyone being naïve enough to ask Red Ned Lynch where he had come by this or that piece of treasure tickled the crowd. "Where did *Ned* get it?" a man cried out mockingly. "Where does Ned Lynch get anything?" another joined in; the tavern exploded with riotous laughter.

Lynch's girl, with one hand massaging the wrenched roots of her hair and the other making a losing effort to keep herself from spilling out of her torn dress, looked up. She made a lightning grab and snatched the brooch from Jane. "*That's* how he got it —you poxy whore!"

She evaded Jane's lunge to retrieve the brooch, tossed it to Ned Lynch, and sprang from her chair, her stiffened, long-nailed fingers clawing at Jane's eyes. Jane grappled with her, knocked the stabbing hand aside, and dealt her a swinging slap on the face. The girl hooked a leg behind Jane's and pushed, falling to the floor on top of her.

As the two women struggled on the floor, the tavern patrons rushed to push back tables and chairs to form a cleared circle. Jane's quick thrust of an elbow into her attacker's midriff was rewarded with a cry of pain and a burst of cheering from the crowd; Lynch's girl retaliated with a blow that banged Jane's head hard against the floor and brought more cheers.

"Six to four on Lynch's whore!" a man called, jingling a handful of coins.

Jane managed to roll over on top of the other girl, grab the shoulders of her dress, and yank downward. The strained fabric ripped, spilling her bosom out—and, more dangerously from her point of view, momentarily hampering her arms.

"Three to one on t'other whore!" another wagerer called, sensing a turn in the course of the struggle.

"That's no whore—that's Sir James's daughter!"

The bettor shrugged. "One man's daughter is another man's whore. The bet remains the same!"

Lynch's girl, her dress in tatters around her waist, scrambled away from Jane and lurched upright, then made a vengeful grab at Jane's dress. At the cost of a disarray of the neckline that would normally have concerned her mightily, Jane regained her feet, and in a highly unladylike but effective manner, ended the fight with a crisp right cross to the girl's jaw that sent her flying over the table and to the floor. The girl either was unconscious or thought it better to pretend to be; in any case, the contest was over.

Nick Debrett looked from the sprawled girl to Jane, who, flushed with exertion and the excitement of battle, was adjusting her ripped dress to some semblance of seemliness, and shook his head wonderingly.

Ned Lynch nodded to her and smiled, then lazily tossed the brooch to her. "You earned it, girl."

"I didn't *earn* it—I *own* it!"

She pressed a catch on the back of the brooch, and the back snapped open. She held it out to Lynch, who read the inscription engraved inside aloud: " 'To my loving daughter, Jane. Father.' " He looked up, confused. "Sir James Barnet was your father?"

"He is yet, no thanks to you!"

Ned Lynch smiled disarmingly. "Dear girl, we are but humble pirates, trying to make do."

"Pirates? Durant's lackeys, that's what you are!" she said scornfully.

Ned Lynch seemed to be turning over in his mind whether to take this as a joke or a mortal insult, but before he arrived at any decision on the matter, a squad of redcoats boiled into the room, scattering the patrons and the furniture as they headed for his table.

They were led by the soldier who had slipped out a few moments before; he pointed at Lynch and his friends, and bawled out, "There he is! Seize him! Seize them all! Their women, too!"

Before he finished speaking, Ned Lynch, Nick Debrett, Mr. Moonbeam, Polonski, and the others were on their feet, their chairs overturned behind them, with cutlasses and daggers out. The melee was joined instantly, and the clash of steel on steel, the grunts of straining swordsmen, the crash of overturning tables and smashed bottles, and the alarmed cries of the patrons filled the air.

While Debrett and Lynch occupied half a dozen soldiers with swordplay, Mr. Moonbeam seemed to prefer greeting his foes with smart blows with bits of broken furniture, and Polonski was content to pick his antagonists up and throw them through the air; after one, or at the most two, such flights, any redcoat was pretty well used up, and no longer a factor in the brawl.

"If ye only had the sense to be as scared as ye should be," Moonbeam called to his friend, "I'm thinkin' yer bowels'd be in wonderful workin' order right now!"

Polonski's reply, as he butted yet another redcoat

in the midriff and smashed the stair rail with him, could have referred equally to his digestive problem or his opinion of his present situation.

A few of the soldiers, with less taste for glory than their fellows, were following their informant's suggestion of seizing the women; slung over the shoulder of one of them, Lynch's girl, even more exposed than she had been when in the same attitude on the *Blarney Cock* the night before, attracted no attention whatever, the tavern customers who might have enjoyed the sight being more concerned with getting out of the way of the fighting.

Two redcoats headed for Jane, who stood bewildered at the confusion around her. One grabbed the brooch from her hand and shouted to a comrade, "Seize the wench!" Two men leaped to the task, their busy hands making it unclear whether they were trying to secure her person or enjoy it.

The man who had won a tidy sum by wagering on Jane's success in the fight with Lynch's girl stepped to her side, slipped a knife into her hand, and withdrew; Jane, in a frenzy of fury and fear, grasped it, and lashed out.

One soldier reeled back, his eyes and mouth reproachfully wide, the dagger protruding just above his belt buckle. Both the wounded man's companion and Jane herself stared at him in awed amazement; then Jane saw another soldier rushing at her with drawn sword raised high. Jane dodged the blow, crouched, grabbed the fallen man's sword, and darted away through the crowd.

"Get the murdering witch!" the soldier who had nearly cleaved her skull yelled. Several soldiers darted toward her, but were diverted by a rush from Mr. Moonbeam and Polonski, whose clubbing and butting tactics effectively kept them from pursuing her.

Ned Lynch and Nick Debrett, holding half a dozen soldiers at bay at the foot of the staircase, with a ring of steel formed by their flickering swords, were momentarily astonished to find that they had been joined by Jane, armed and evidently ready to fight.

Wedged together on the staircase, the men's rough-and-tumble tactics—including kicking at whatever vulnerable parts presented themselves, and throwing whatever came to hand—combined with Jane's skilled fencing-school approach, provided a good defense; but the very press of numbers of the soldiers forced them steadily backward, up the stairs.

"I'd figured on going upstairs anyhow," Debrett called to Lynch, "but not under these circumstances!"

"Well, now, and isn't it just as much fun to be having a fine row with the brutal and licentious soldiery as to be bedding a lass in our host's hired rooms?"

Debrett shook his head and grinned. Ned Lynch was just crazy enough to mean it.

Jane, her sword darting and parrying constantly, its tip now glistening red, gritted her teeth. How had it come about that she was fighting for her life against her country's troops, side-by-side with a pair of rogues who bantered bawdry in the face of death?

They were now at the landing, and Ned Lynch suddenly turned aside to face the threat of a soldier who had sought to outflank them by avoiding the stairs and hauling himself directly up by the balcony railing. Keeping the man off with the fastest sword work he could manage, he groped behind him, found a doorknob, turned it, and stepped backward; the soldier lunged and followed him through the door before he could close it.

The noise and cries from below had not distracted the young man and woman in the bedroom. Allowed only one trip to town a month from his family's hill plantation by his stern father, the man spent the intervening time by planning in loving detail everything he wanted to crowd into his one-day vacation, during which he never left his regular bedroom at the Bull's Foot; the woman, appreciating him as a regular and enthusiastic customer, was equally absorbed.

It was not until the door of the room was flung open and two men bent on killing each other burst into it, their swords slashing within inches of the couple's heads, that they abandoned their occupation and huddled under the thin coverlet.

Ned Lynch moved past the bed, toward the window, then feinted sideways as the soldier followed him, darted back to the bed, hooked the coverlet on the point of his cutlass, and flung it over his opponent's head as though netting a huge fish.

While the soldier thrashed helplessly, Ned Lynch spun him around, winding him as tightly as in a cocoon, then briskly kicked him through the open window. "Maybe all that cloth'll break the poor fellow's fall," he murmured. "Then again, maybe not. . . ."

He turned and raised his sword in a salute to the two bare figures entwined on the bed, frozen like statues in nearly the ultimate moment of their love-making. "Thank you," he said briskly. "Carry on!"

He backed to the window just as three more soldiers rushed into the room, then stopped, struck by the sight of the lovers, who, though not yet able to follow Ned's suggestion, had still not untangled themselves. The soldiers' pause gave Ned the chance to spring to the windowsill, where he stood poised briefly, then vanished—not, to their surprise, leaping into the street, but upward, as he grasped some outside projection and raised himself out of sight.

On the hallway landing, Jane and Debrett were yielding ground to the soldiers, and had backed into a corner. Debrett felt behind him and discovered two doors, but the knobs of both failed to turn in his urgent grasp; evidently they were locked. The soldiers moved forward, and it seemed certain that the fiercely battling girl and black man would be overpowered.

The skylight over their head shattered, showering everyone with fragments of glass, and Ned Lynch plummeted onto the soldiers, his leather boots scattering them like tenpins.

In the sudden lull that ensued as the soldiers tried to collect themselves, Nick Debrett whirled and slammed his foot against the nearest door. It burst open, and he grabbed Jane Barnet and dragged her through it. Ned Lynch drove back the three dazed soldiers still on their feet with a flurry of cuts and thrusts of his cutlass, then backed in after his friend.

"Hold them off at the door just a moment, there's a good lad," he called to Debrett, then raced to where Jane stood by the room's window and lifted her out onto the ledge outside it. Once sure she was safely placed, he vaulted out beside her.

Jane looked down to the alley twenty feet below and shuddered. The cobblestones were far away, but it seemed to her that she could see every one of them distinctly, and they all looked sharp, hard, and unwelcoming.

Ned Lynch whistled a fast tune between his teeth and looked toward the next building. It was level with them, but too far for a standing jump, even for him, and out of the question for the girl, but . . . He reached for the edge of the roof just above him and grabbed at the rain gutter—a half-log, hollowed out, that ran the length of the building. One determined tug brought it away at one end; another completely detached it from the building, although its weight nearly flicked him off the ledge. He placed one end of the gutter against the wall and swung the other carefully across the gap that separated them from the roof of the next building. Jane looked at it with horror. It was all too clear what Ned Lynch meant to do, and meant her to do—and it did not seem possible.

Ned ran spryly across the improvised bridge, stepped off it on the other side, and turned to Jane with a reassuring wave. "Come on, it's easy."

Jane glanced behind her. Nick Debrett had been forced back nearly to the window by the two soldiers attacking him. He risked a glance at her, saw the wrenched-off gutter spanning the gap between the buildings, and called, "Hurry! Make room for me!"

Jane looked across at Lynch, then down at the street—no softer than the last time she'd seen it, but worth risking, when she considered what falling into the hands of the soldiers would mean—took a deep breath, and stepped out onto the frail gutter.

She was careful not to look down, only ahead at

the gutter, which seemed not much wider than a rope, and at Ned Lynch, who had now crouched to hold and steady it.

He smiled encouragement at Jane. As she slowly drew closer to him, she was aware that he was positively enjoying this moment of supreme danger; and the thought flickered across her mind that, in some strange way, underneath the anger and fear, so was she. . . .

Just short of the roof, she set a foot down off-center, and the gutter rolled—not very much, but enough to pitch her off. As she began to fall, she hurled herself forward, grabbing at the hand Lynch extended. Her hands clasped around it, and, swinging from his arm, she slammed bruisingly into the side of the building, then hung there. Slowly, taking her full weight on one arm, Ned Lynch drew her up and over the edge of the roof. She sprawled, panting.

"Come on, Nick!" Lynch yelled cheerfully. "No time for games!"

Back in the bedroom, Nick Debrett gave an exasperated grimace at his captain's choice of words, then flexed his knees and sprang at his opponents, letting out a lionlike roar. The disconcerted soldiers stumbled back toward the doorway, giving Debrett the chance to turn, run to the window, and, almost in one motion, leap through it and dart along the gutter to the roof where Lynch and Jane waited.

"What kept you, lad?" Lynch said, grinning.

Debrett shook his head in distress. "Come on, you crazy fool!"

Ned Lynch grapped Jane's hand and pulled her to her feet. Then he looked back at the window by which they had left and saw the two soldiers peering at them. He bent down and picked up a round stone the size of a small apple from the roof and placed it under the end of the gutter. "Not likely those lads'll venture on our little bridge, but if they do, this'll see to it that they'll go tumbling down, bridge and all!"

He gave a whoop of sheer pleasure and excitement,

and set off at a run after Debrett, dragging Jane with him.

They halted at the far side of the roof and looked down. They were above the street market, and gaily striped awnings over the stalls seemed to stretch beneath them like a sea.

Ned Lynch surveyed the scene, and cocked an ear for the sounds of pursuit; they could hear confused orders being bawled in the next street, and it would be only a matter of moments before their hunters had them at bay.

He cast another glance downward, as if making a rapid calculation. "Well, not a second to lose, as they say." He grabbed Jane about the waist, lifted her from her feet, held her poised over the edge of the roof, and let her drop.

Chapter 9

Jane had time for one short, piercing scream of fear and outrage as she dropped. Then it seemed as if she were slapped heavily on the back and bounced briefly upward, like a tennis ball rebounding from the net. She was on her back on a billowing striped surface—a market-stall awning, she realized.

She glared up at the roof, twenty feet above. Lynch and Debrett were peering down interestedly at her.

Ned Lynch was delighted. "It works!" Jane caught the words and wondered bitterly what he would have said if it *hadn't* worked, and she'd smashed on the pavement like a thrown egg. Probably something like "No use in trying that, then— we'll have to think of something else."

"Here, you next," he said to Debrett.

Nick was firm on that point. "Not me, mate!"

"Then both of us at once. Come on!" He grabbed Debrett's hand and jumped; Debrett gave a startled yell as he was pulled over the edge.

Jane shut her eyes as the falling pirates came down, seemingly on top of her; she felt the impact as they hit the canvas; then there was a tearing sound, a feeling of falling, and a curiously soft landing.

She opened her eyes and found that she and her companions were in the middle of a huge display of fresh fish; above her, the tattered awning let in a long stretch of bright-blue sky.

Jane sat up and indignantly grappled with a large fish that had been driven down the front of her dress by the force of her fall; then, slipping and slithering on the mound of fish, she tried to get to her feet.

"There they are! After them!" The cry came from soldiers only a few stalls away. The three fugitives scrambled away from the ruined fish stall and ran across the marketplace; Debrett hung back a moment to fling a dozen fish into their pursuers' path, and had the satisfaction of seeing at least two of them skid and take heavy falls.

"Stop those people! Stop them!" a raging soldier yelled. But the seemingly aimless crowd somehow contrived to drift out of the way of the fleeing men and the girl with them, and to drift back in time to impede the soldiers chasing them.

Debrett, Lynch, and Jane pounded past the tavern. Mr. Moonbeam, Polonski, and others of the *Blarney Cock*'s crew emerged as they passed, saw the pursuing soldiers, and ran forward. Polonski dived, arms spread wide, and brought three redcoats down, bounded up and butted another in the midsection, and made off down the street. Mr. Moonbeam passed among the dazed soldiers with a few well-aimed jabs and clouts from a chair leg, and joined him.

At the end of the street stood a wagon piled high with stalks of bananas. The driver was perched up front, holding his team steady, evidently waiting for customers for his fruit. Ned ran for the wagon, sprang to a bench, then to a table, and up onto the seat alongside the driver, who, not stopping to ask questions, leaped into the street.

Lynch leaned down and waved. "Thanks, mate!"

Debrett lifted Jane and tossed her up onto the bananas, and vaulted up to land beside her, his impact bursting at least a dozen of them. "Go!" he called.

Ned Lynch cracked the reins and gave a long, keening yell that started the horses off at a gallop. The wagon's owner was in a frenzy of rage. "Stop, thief! Stop, I say! Come back here at once! That's—"

His tirade was stopped by the arrival of the soldiers, whose determination to catch their quarry made them disinclined to step aside for mere citizens; he was bowled over and sent rolling along the cobblestones.

One soldier ran for his tethered horse, calling, "After them! After them! Get the horses! Sound the alarm!"

He prepared to mount and lead the pursuit, but in his haste missed the stirrup, slipped, and fell flat on his face.

The wagon, moving at the speed of a fast stage-coach, careered down the street, not turning aside for the market stalls in its way. Its progress was accompanied by the sound of rending wood, smashing wares, and the groans and curses of the proprietors.

"Nick!"

"Aye!" Debrett said, clutching the edge of the wagon to keep from being jolted off.

"Must remember to pay for the damage! Can't have our fun at these good people's expense!"

Debrett threw him a sour look, then turned to Jane. He shouted over the rumble of the wagon, now moving more rapidly than it had ever been designed to, "Thank you, ma'am."

"I fought for *my* life, not yours!" Jane snapped. With her neck in danger at every jolt of the wagon, her body bruised in front from her impact with the wall of the building they had escaped to, and still stinging in back from her descent to the awning, and her dress in barely decent tatters and coated with fish slime and pulped banana, she was in no mood for friendliness from the men she blamed for her predicament.

Debrett stared at her for a moment, then shrugged. "Thank you, anyway."

Three miles outside of Kingston, the wagon had not slackened its pace, though the racing horses were now covered with lather as they responded to Ned Lynch's passionate efforts to urge them on. He frowned; they were good beasts, but much longer at this pace, and they'd be good for nothing any more.

In the rear, Nick Debrett peeled and ate a banana, then offered one to Jane, who only glared and hung on as tightly as she could. Then she looked past him at the road behind them and gestured urgently.

He turned, to see a dozen mounted soldiers round a bend in the road and gallop in pursuit. They were no more than a hundred yards off.

Jane and Debrett exchanged glances, then grabbed stalks of bananas and began tossing them over the tail-gate and into the road, where some of them burst satisfyingly.

To their disgust, none of the thundering horses slipped and fell. "Why would that be?" Debrett said. "A human being, now, if there's a banana skin on the street, he'll go head-over-heels, every time. Why doesn't it work the same with horses?"

Jane, with poisonous sweetness, said, "What a fascinating scientific question. Why don't you write to the Royal Society about it?"

Debrett ignored this and shouted forward. "Ned!"

"I hear you, Nick!"

"Company!"

Ned Lynch glanced over his shoulder and took in the oncoming troops, now definitely gaining on them with every pace. With his own team already slowing, they would be caught in a matter of minutes. He gave a sharp glance to the country at the left side of the road. If he remembered aright . . .

"Hold on, mates! We're going to take a shortcut!" He reined the horses violently leftward; Jane shrieked as the wagon slewed into the turn and heeled over on two wheels, spilling bananas into the roadway and sending her sliding dangerously near the edge. A bone-breaking bounce that had her and Nick Debrett momentarily in the air marked their passage over the ditch alongside the road, and then they were jolting over a rough field.

Guiding the horses around trees and other obstacles with speed and sureness, Ned Lynch was having the time of his life. At any moment, the soldiers might catch up with them, or the wagon strike a rock that would split it apart, breaking all their necks. It was grand fun.

His two passengers were less exhilarated; they clung desperately to the sides of the wagon, and could feel an ominous wrenching and shifting of its boards at each new jolt, warning that it was on the point of falling apart.

A slight downward motion, a giant spray of water on either side of the wagon, and a brief climb indicated that they had just passed through a small, winding stream.

A shout came from their driver. "Nick!"

"What?"

"Ask the lady if she can swim."

Debrett began to wonder if his friend's wits had started to wander, from all the jouncing. "What?"

"Ask her if she knows how to swim! To swim!" To Debrett's horror, Ned Lynch dropped the reins for an instant and pantomimed a breaststroke in the air, then picked them up again.

"Why?"

Lynch did not bother to answer. Holding on to the edge of the seat with one hand, he leaned forward and reached down. By stretching as far as he could, he was just able to touch the wrought-iron pin that held the tongue—to which the horses' traces were attached—to the front axle, and began to tug at it. Glancing ahead, he could see a glint of blue through the rapidly approaching screen of trees—the ocean. There was their goal and their refuge—and Lynch could even see the *Blarney Cock,* riding easily at anchor a quarter of a mile out. Unfortunately, the shoreline here was a little different from that of the gentle cove where he and Nick had conducted Folly; there was a little matter of a cliff the height of three houses or so piled on each other to be dealt with. . . .

Fortunately for what remained of their nerves, Jane's and Debrett's attention was held by the soldiers, now bare yards away, close enough for their rage-distorted faces to be seen clearly.

Ten yards from the edge of the cliff, Ned Lynch managed to work the iron pin loose. He wrenched at the reins and dropped them; the freed horses veered to the right, only just managing to avoid galloping over the edge.

The wagon plunged straight ahead, its momentum carrying it well away from the cliff. Ned Lynch bawled "Jump!" and hurled himself to one side; Jane and Nick Debrett, suddenly finding themselves in a flying machine, did the same.

Jane twisted in the air and managed to get herself head downward with arms extended just before she hit the water. She split the surface cleanly and descended nearly to the sandy bottom, then slowly rose. The water was littered with an almost solid layer of bananas, broken by splintered fragments of the wagon—and by two faces grinning at her.

"You are a madman!" Jane gasped, treading water. She was uneasily aware that there seemed to be rather less of her dress than there had been before the plunge.

Ned Lynch raised his eyebrows in acknowledgement. "Yes, madam. But a live one, at least!"

"Best we try to stay that way, Ned," Nick Debrett said, pointing at the top of the cliff above them. Most of the soldiers peering over the edge were evidently too dumbfounded to take any action; but they could see that one had unslung his musket and was aiming at them. A cloud of smoke drifted from the barrel an instant before they heard the report; a banana some distance away leaped from the water and fell back.

Lynch looked calculatingly at the tiny figures of the troopers. "At that distance and angle, there's no chance they could hit us. However, we'll be on our way. Shouldn't think we'd have to swim the whole distance, though—now that the soldier laddies are shooting, some of the crew'll hear it and come to see what's up."

And, true enough, a longboat was even now being lowered from the *Blarney Cock*.

"Since we must swim for it," Lynch observed cheerfully, "how about a little sporting flutter on the result—first aboard the longboat is the winner!"

Chapter 10

Far out to sea, the *Blarney Cock* ran before a fresh breeze that bellied its sails, gently ruffled Jane Barnet's hair, and pressed her tattered but drying dress to her body as she stood at the rail near the bow. Forward of her, at the beakhead, Polonski stood, watched intently by the perched rooster; behind her, some of the crew, under Mr. Moonbeam's direction, were painting the deck red; others had laid aside their tasks and were looking at her with frank interest.

Nick Debrett, now dressed in fresh clothes, appeared from a hatchway behind the knot of men in time to hear one of them mutter, "Lovely bit o' padding for a sailor's hammock, ain't she?"

Debrett stepped in front of them, his one eye staring pointedly at their empty hands. He did not, however, reprove them for being delinquent in their duties, but said gently, "Fancy the lass, do you?"

"Aye, Mr. Debrett, that we do," the man who had spoken said.

"And it's no wonder. A lovely creature she is, to be sure."

Encouraged by the man-to-man tone of the conversation so far, another sailor spoke up. "I'd give a pretty penny to spend an hour with that, I'll tell you."

"*Would* you?"

"Aye, I would indeed. A pretty penny." The sailor wagged his head and grinned.

"The question," Debrett said, even more gently, "is, would you be willing to give your *life* for it?"

The crewmen looked at him nervously.

"I'll tell you once, and only once, so listen sharp. She's not a 'lass' and not a 'that' and not a toy to play with. She's a *lady*. And if any man is to fool with her, 'twill be your captain. Do you take my point?"

Nick Debrett looked menacingly at the hastily dispersing crewmen, then with concern toward Jane. His face was set and worried as he turned and walked away.

Jane, unaware of any of this, looked out over the sea to where Jamaica lay like a low green cloud on the horizon. There was something soothing about being this far away from the island and the troubles and worries it now held for her. Even her concern for her parents, and her smoldering hatred for Lord Durant, seemed less urgent out here. She felt that she could begin to understand the lure the sea held for such men as Ned Lynch. . . . She was suddenly aware of the presence of Lynch himself behind her, and turned to face him. One hand involuntarily moved to her hair to straighten it; then she halted the gesture, angry with herself—what need had she to make herself neat for this scoundrel? And in any case, there would be little use to the effort, she reflected ruefully; she had restored her dress to decency, but it was definitely and irrevocably a ruin. And—damn the man!—what right had he to smile at her?

"How long have you been standing there?" she asked coldly.

"Not very long."

"You move quietly." Her tone did not make it a compliment.

"Do I?"

"It's natural among thieves," Jane said with false sweetness.

Ned Lynch was stung. "Begging your pardon, madam, but I am not a thief. I am a pirate, and proud to be called one."

"Will you return my family possessions?"

"I will not."

She shrugged and spread her hands. "Well, then, there it is: you're a thief."

The topic of the Barnet treasure was beginning to bore Ned. He had taken it in the legitimate practice of his trade, a piece of land piracy more cleverly brought off than many of his sea fights, and had distributed it fairly among his crew as prescribed by custom. It was a dead issue, no matter what Miss Barnet thought of it. "As you wish. Now, why do you talk like a French girl?" Jane's accent had, from time to time, even during the mad events of the fight at the tavern and the chase afterward, popped into his mind as a puzzling circumstance.

Jane ignored his question, considering it a feeble attempt at social conversation she had no intention of encouraging. "Am I your prisoner?"

"Do you feel like a prisoner?"

"I am unable to leave of my own free will," she said.

"I was not aware that you'd requested it," Ned Lynch said blandly. "You shall be put ashore in the morning—if that is your wish."

"It is."

"Consider it done, then." There was a mocking undertone in his ready agreement that Jane did not understand. "I have no reason to hold you here against your will. I trust that you will find the company of soldiers more to your liking."

Jane frowned. "What do you mean by that?"

"What I mean, ma'am, is that you are a fugitive." With relish, he ticked off the reasons for this on the fingers of one hand. "Item, you fought the King's army in the company of buccaneers. Item, you joined in the theft of a wagonload of bananas and its destruction, even though the same was accomplished by one of the said buccaneers. Item, you destroyed property in the shape of a market awning by jumping on it." Lynch grinned at Jane's indignant snort. "Item, in that unsavory brawl in the tavern, you slipped a dagger into the brisket of one poor lad. In the eyes of the law, you're as much a criminal as I am."

"I fought only in my own defense!" Jane said hotly. "As for that other nonsense . . ."

Ned Lynch smiled smugly. "You needn't excuse yourself to me, girl. Only to Lord Durant. Good day." He made an overly graceful bow, turned, and made his way aft.

Jane looked after him, resenting deeply the fact that he was dead right. It was one thing to cherish a dream of vengeance against Lord Durant, waiting one's opportunity to strike. It was quite another to be on the special list of malefactors attracting My Lord's personal attention. And how detestable of Red Ned Lynch to make her see it!

"Now, isn't it strange, Nick," Lynch said some hours later, facing Debrett across the richly laden dining table in his quarters, "that even though we're pirates, men that have forsworn the laws of God and man—and aren't so sure about those of chance—here we are, eating our evening meal at the hour every peasant and householder is? We might have been hungry as the devil himself in the middle of the afternoon, but would either of us go to that fancy cook we captured off that French ship and tell him to do us up a dinner? Never! Why is it, d'you suppose, that we eat at much the same time—and eat much the same things, come to think of it—each day, and the same with answering the calls of nature, barring poor Polonski of course? Are we free men, then, or a sort of clockworks?" He looked deeply into the silver goblet, souvenir of a captured French ship, as if for an answer, sighed, and gulped the red wine it held.

Nick Debrett ignored his friend's venture into philosophy, which he recognized as Lynch's way of avoiding bringing up something he was reluctant to discuss.

Lynch finally squinted across at him and said, "Did the girl eat, then?"

Debrett shook his head. "Refused."

Lynch scowled, seemingly at the innocent goblet. "Stubborn."

"Spoiled."

The two men ate in silence for a while; then Debrett looked across the table with concern. "You fancy her, don't you, Ned?"

"Me?" Lynch's look around the cabin, as if to see if Debrett might have been addressing someone else with such a preposterous notion, was not convincing.

"A woman's place is between the sheets. I suspect there's more to this wench than that."

"The girl leaves in the morning," Ned Lynch said firmly.

"I hope so, Ned. Because something tells me that if she remains, we head for shipwreck . . . as they say."

Ned Lynch looked thoughtfully at Debrett and wiped a smear of grease from the corner of his mouth. "How long have we sailed together, Nick?"

"Six years."

"Closer to seven. Did I ever let you down, Nick, in those seven years?"

"Have I ever said so?"

"You gave me your trust, and I gave you a ship to call your own, and together we've sailed this ocean and done as we pleased, and no one has ever dared stand in our way more than once." He looked keenly at Nick Debrett. "Do you trust me now, Nick?"

Debrett sighed and nodded. "With my life, yes. But it isn't *my* life that worries me, only yours. That girl is trouble, Ned. A pirate in love is like a fish out of water: both are where they shouldn't be. But only the fish has sense enough to know it."

Ned Lynch's face tightened. Damnation, but old Nick was pushing this a trifle far! The man was seeing shoals and reefs that weren't there, with his lunatic notion that Ned Lynch was losing his heart to a bad-tempered slip of a girl . . . though, by God, she was a dab at the swordplay, and didn't look bad at all, with the dress half off her or plastered to her body. . . .

"The girl leaves in the morning," he said shortly.

Nick Debrett's expression was not as trustful as Ned would have liked, but he nodded and turned back to his food.

As the *Blarney Cock*'s longboat approached the deserted beach—as near to Kingston as she could be landed without attracting notice—Jane was nervous. Before yesterday's wild adventures, her situation had been dark enough. Now, with all the forces of the law doubtless seeking her, it was desperate. She looked, unseeing, at the vividly white beach and green forest, and felt a sudden inward sinking when the boat grated on the sand. Unpleasant as the interlude on the *Blarney Cock* had been, it was over now, and she had a sea of worries and dangers to face. For a moment she wished that the abominable Captain Lynch had in fact held her prisoner—it would be almost a relief not to be able to do anything, to have to depend on someone else's will. . . . She pushed the thought firmly away and stood up.

Ned Lynch sprang onto the beach and offered a hand to help her out of the longboat; Nick Debrett joined them.

Lynch gave Jane a crooked smile and waved expansively around the landscape. "The freedom you wanted, girl. Enjoy it—while you can."

She glared at him, then turned without a word and began walking through the clinging sand to the woods. Lynch grabbed a sword from one of the longboat's crew and hailed Jane, "Mademoiselle!"

When she turned, he held the sword up. "I would be remiss were I to leave you defenseless." He tossed the sword toward her; it turned once in the air, and the hilt thumped into her outstretched palm. A flash of anger warmed her—he was so sure of himself! If he had miscalculated his throw, or her response to it, the sword would have spitted her. But that seemed to be Captain Lynch's way—make a decision and carry it out without thinking twice. She hefted the sword, instinctively falling into a fencing stance.

Ned Lynch grinned. "Do I detect a certain hostility, madam? You fancy running me through?"

"I would indeed—thief!"

Lynch's grin grew broader. He stepped back, drew his own sword, and brought it up. *"En garde,* then."

Jane tightened her grip on her borrowed weapon, raised it to the formal upright position, and fixed him with a cold stare.

The sight of the slight girl in the stained and tattered dress, tense with anger, poised on the bright sand in the classic position of a schooled fencer, might have struck some as touching, others as almost beautiful; Ned Lynch and his companions found it comic, and burst into laughter.

"Methinks the lady is about to paint a picture, Captain Lynch," Debrett observed with mock solemnity.

The laughter continued, enraging Jane further. She extended her sword and lunged for Ned Lynch. Not bothering to parry, he stepped aside, then brought his sword up inside her guard. She stopped suddenly, and found the tip of Lynch's blade resting lightly on her bosom. It gave one twitch, slicing the cord that fastened her dress at the neck, and she felt a rush of air as the cloth fell partly away.

"Lesson number one," Lynch said softly. "Do not get provoked."

Jane knocked his sword aside; both stepped back one pace and brought their swords up again. They circled each other; Jane thrust and was parried, then defended herself against a cut from Lynch; the exchange continued. It seemed almost on even terms, but Jane was instantly aware that Lynch was toying with her, that the skill she had so painfully acquired in her fencing classes was no real defense against his experience.

Lynch suddenly dipped his sword to the sand; before she could take advantage of this for a lunging attack, he flicked it upward, showering sand into her face. She stumbled back, desperately trying to scrub the grit from her eyes.

"Lesson number two: forget fair play when you fight for your life."

Blind rage banished Jane's learned techniques from her mind and gave her a momentary advantage as she heedlessly slashed at Lynch, the fury of her attack driving him back a pace or so. He sidestepped and tripped her, then gave her backside a slap with his sword as she stumbled by. She crashed to her knees and felt her sword wrenched from her hand—Ned Lynch had stepped on the blade and was standing over her. He was not grinning in triumph now, but looked at her quite seriously.

"Lesson number three: never raise your sword to Ned Lynch unless you are prepared to die."

If there had been a way to make sure of Lynch's death at the same time, Jane would almost have been willing to settle for that.

He reached down to help her rise. She pushed his hand away and got to her feet. She was breathing hard from exertion and rage, her backside still stung from Lynch's slap. Her knees were scraped from her fall to the sand, and her ruined dress was open almost to the waist, but the look of disdain she gave him was regal.

Ned Lynch picked up the fallen sword and held it out to her. "Keep it. You'll find use for it, I guarantee."

She ignored him, turned, and walked away into the green line of forest at the edge of the beach.

"A proud lady, that one," Mr. Moonbeam said, making sure Jane was out of earshot before he spoke; he had no desire to prompt her to a stinging reply.

Ned Lynch said nothing, but gazed at her dwindling figure with an intentness that gave Nick Debrett a strong feeling of foreboding. There had been passion in that fight on both sides, and the passion of hate and combat could too easily, Debrett knew, be transformed to something else.

Chapter 11

Just over twenty-four hours after she had left it, Jane returned to the shabby boardinghouse on the waterfront. The journey from the beach to town had been tiresome, but the last stage, threading her way through the slum quarter, had been nerve-racking, as she had slipped through the mean streets with face averted, dreading a cry of recognition or a challenge from a soldier.

She saw the landlady on the pavement outside the house, haggling with a street vendor, and concealed herself behind a carriage. She was in no mood to encounter the spiteful old woman, and if the word had truly been spread about her role in the fight yesterday, the landlady would doubtless be eager to turn her in to the authorities in the hope of a reward, or merely out of malice.

The woman went inside. Jane waited a moment, then darted for the doorway. Out of nowhere, it seemed, a ragged street tumbler appeared and cartwheeled around her, holding out his hand. "Spare a coin for a poor man out of your charity, mistress," he whined mockingly, delighted to see someone even more tattered of clothing than he was. Jane brushed past him, pleased that at least she had not been recognized.

She crept up the warped staircase to the second floor and entered the dingy room. Explanations and apologies rose to her lips—though goodness knew how she could possibly tell the whole bizarre story!—as she saw her mother sitting on the lumpy bed. Then her heart leaped as she saw the other occupant of the room, a darkly handsome man with an expression of deep concern.

Jane rushed to embrace him, and yielded gratefully to the strength and comfort of his arms. "I'm so glad to see you," she murmured, pressing her face against the sturdy material of his coat. "Dear, *dear* Willard . . ."

Lord Durant's secretary held the daughter of the man his master had imprisoned and robbed close to him.

After a long moment, she gave a shuddering sigh, freed herself, and turned to Lady Barnet. "Mother, I—"

Her mother held up a hand, stopping her. "Tell me later, Jane. Willard has something to tell us—something very important."

The streets were comparatively uncrowded in the early afternoon, and Jane felt safe enough in venturing out, dressed plainly and with a handkerchief held up to her face as if to mask somewhat the odors the insistent sun drew from the street refuse. It took all her courage to peer through the door of the Bull's Foot tavern; but there were no raucous shouts of greeting, and, thank God, no soldiers present. She looked to the center of the room, and, as she had hoped, there was Nick Debrett, at least; his captain could not be far off. He was bouncing one amply endowed girl on his knee and was closely flanked by two others. Jane looked around, but could not find Ned Lynch.

Choked laughter from the staircase drew her glance. A drunken seaman, his clothes evidently just pulled on, was being supported down the stairs by a highly amused woman in a flimsy shift. Jane's lips tightened. Of course! That famous second floor, with its nearly endless row of well-tenanted bedrooms. That was where Lynch would be, for a certainty! Well, he would have to interrupt his swinish pleasures for a moment. It might even be that he would be glad to, since she had a nice bit of business to put in his way, and doubtless his thieving instincts were as strong as his lust!

At the landing, she paused and looked reminiscently at the still-unrepaired skylight through which Ned Lynch had plunged. In spite of herself, a faint smile appeared on her lips—it had been terrifying and horrible, but, *bon Dieu,* it was something to remember, that fight!

She was now faced with half a dozen closed doors. Presumably Lynch was occupied behind one of them. She tried the nearest.

The energetic movements beneath the rumpled bedsheet made clear what was in progress, but not the participants. Then a reproving cry—"Hey, lass, 'tis not a piece o' sugar cane ye're dealin' with!"—delivered with a strong Irish lilt told her that the prime mover was Mr. Moonbeam, not Ned.

She approached the next door cautiously, and squinted through the crack between it and the jamb.

Ned Lynch was sprawled on the bed, its top sheet pulled up to his waist. He was sweaty, his hair disordered, his eyes glazed. Jane deduced that his state was due more to the half-empty rum bottle and the mug of it he was gulping than to the woman who sat on the bed beside him, clad only in a rumpled underskirt, combing her hair. With that much grog in him, Jane estimated, he wasn't likely to be much use to the woman right now; she only hoped his head would be clear enough for what she had to propose. She stepped back and kicked the door open.

"You?" he said thickly, trying to focus on her.

"Me."

The woman made the futile gesture of tugging her skirt down to cover her knees—with everything below them, and above the waist, uncovered, it seemed to Jane to be hardly worth the effort and spoke up indignantly. "Here, now, who the devil do you think you are, walking in on a person's privacy!"

Ned Lynch seemed to pull himself together; when he spoke, his voice was a trifle clearer, and he even managed to regain his customary offensive tone of light mockery. "No need for that. This lady here is probably just wanting another fencing lesson."

The whore was dubious. "Fencing lesson? Here?" She was sure he was wrong—you had fencing lessons at a school or some such, not in one of the Bull's Foot bedrooms. She looked at Jane suspiciously.

"I want your help," she told Lynch.

He choked on the rum he was swallowing.

"I'll just bet she does," the whore said. Doubtless "fencing lessons" was some sort of thieves' talk for something special in the bedroom line, and this fancy piece was offering it to Red Ned. She felt aggrieved; it was hard enough for a working girl without amateur competition pushing in.

"Help for what? Charity work?" Lynch asked cuttingly. He nudged the woman next to him. "Educated in Paris, she was," he confided to her. "Can you picture it? Comes back with a lot of heartwarming notions about the downtrodden and the underprivileged. But then, when you don't have to spend your days working, you can spend them thinking." He turned to Jane. "Well, in case you've not heard, Mademoiselle Barnet, I myself have been retired from Christian virtue many a long year."

He lounged back on the bolster behind him, peered angrily at Jane over the rim of the mug, and tousled his woman's hair.

She cackled and said, "That's right, love, you tell her!"

Jane gave him a level look. "It *is* . . . charity work."

"*Good* day, Miss Barnet." Lynch lowered his hand from the whore's hair to her bosom and gave it a friendly squeeze, an unmistakable signal that he considered his interview with Jane at an end.

She ignored this and continued, "*But* it is paid."

"Paid, then? The reward to be reaped in heaven, no doubt."

The woman next to him evidently considered this highly witty, and guffawed and slapped the man on the shoulder.

"The reward to be collected on the night."

Ned Lynch stared at her owlishly, stuck a finger in his ear and probed it, a gesture that said more clearly that he was beginning to doubt whether it was functioning properly. A massive belch bubbled up from his throat, and he looked pleased; his woman laughed harder than ever.

"There is no trouble with your hearing, Captain Lynch," Jane said icily. "It is only your bedside manners that are in need of repair."

"What a clever female she is, don't you agree?" Ned asked his companion, tracing out a spiral design with one finger on her breast. "A real credit to her species, whichever one that might be."

"Are you interested or not?"

Lynch sighed and belched again. Dear God, the woman wouldn't be driven away. "What is the work?"

Jane glanced at the disheveled whore, who seemed on the point of starting up her trade with Lynch without concern for the visitor's presence. "Not in front of her."

"Well, just who in the name of the Almighty do you think you are? You think you can just dance into somebody's bedroom and insult people like that!" The woman disengaged herself from Lynch's grip and advanced on Jane. Lynch, seeing Jane's grim face, hauled her back, saying, "There, there, calm yourself." If Jane Barnet went on battering his women, he reflected, he'd soon run out of them, and wouldn't that be a pity? "Here, now, just put your pretty little fingers in your pretty little ears. That way you won't be hearing anything you shouldn't. That's right, that's good. Now, stay just like that for a minute." Satisfied that the woman was temporarily deaf enough, he looked up at Jane. "All right, what's the work?"

Jane took a deep breath. "Kill Durant."

Ned Lynch stared at her in astonishment, then clapped his hands over the whore's ears, pinning her fingers there. By God, the Barnet girl was right—this wasn't stuff to be spoken of before anyone who might carry tales!

"The pay," Jane continued, "is ten thousand doubloons."

Lynch was suddenly sober. "By whose word?"

"Willard Culverwell, Durant's personal secretary, your friend, and my cousin."

"Your cousin, is he?" Ned nodded thoughtfully. That explained much—why Durant's man would be willing to work against him, as he had by signaling Major Folly's departure with the chest. A Barnet connection, he would naturally be hot for undercutting their enemy. Lynch felt a slight sense of relief; it had troubled him that Culverwell would betray the man whose pay he took, but if it was a matter of a family feud, that made it all regular.

Jane explained. "Everything Durant has stolen, his entire fortune, is to be placed on a ship for England. And Durant will be there himself to see it done."

"When?" Lynch demanded.

"Tonight."

"Tonight!"

Jane saw in the whore's face a dawning awareness that something interesting was being discussed, and a tensing of her arms, as if she were about to wrench her fingers loose from Lynch's grip; she nodded to him, and he increased the pressure of his hands. The whore glared sullenly but relaxed.

"*Ten thousand* doubloons, Captain Lynch."

"I heard you the first time, Miss Barnet." He ran over in his mind what he would need to know. "How many men will Durant have on hand?"

"Fifty."

"This fact also from Cousin Willard?"

"Yes."

Lynch ruminated a moment, then squinted up at her. "You wouldn't be trying to make a fool of me, would you, Miss Barnet?"

Jane looked at him with an elaborately polite disclaiming glance. "I would have no need to do that, Captain Lynch."

She and the pirate exchanged glares as the other woman struggled under Lynch's grip; but both of them knew that, in spite of their mutual antipathy, a bargain had been struck.

The *Blarney Cock*'s mascot rooster peered intently, like a nearsighted judge in an incongruously bright-colored wig, at Ned Lynch. What the hell was the fowl staring at? he wondered. Moonbeam's damned bird always had that close-watching look about it; maybe it was a spy for Durant, and the droppings that whitened its perch were a sort of code message that could be read from shore by a telescope. Now, there was a crazy idea for you—but the bird *did* have that informer's look about it. . . .

He knew that the strange fancy he was entertaining was his mind's way of keeping him from dwelling on the action planned for this night; not that he was nervous about it, strictly speaking, but it didn't do to brood over it and start reexamining the plan. The thing to do was figure it right the first time, and put the whole thing away until the time came.

He watched a youthful pirate lacing the thong that secured his cutlass scabbard to his shoulder belt. The lad, feeling his captain's eyes on him, hurried the job, and was left poking the end of the thong at a hole it would not fit into.

"At ease, Harold," Lynch said. "We've got till darkness before we move."

The boy smiled weakly, but still mechanically tried to fumble the thong into the wrong hole. Lynch made a mental note to see that he was kept on the edge of the action tonight; good stuff in him, but he needed seasoning.

It was almost sunset, and the shadows were long on the *Blarney Cock*'s deck. Ned Lynch passed among his men, checking their work, patting some on the back, exchanging a jest with others. It was good that they had their tasks to do, he thought—seeing to the sails and rigging, sharpening swords and daggers, cleaning muskets and small arms, measuring powder, making sure of their flints. As always, a small party was painting the deck red. That was the way of it on ships; when you finished a job, going from fore to aft, by the time you reached aft, it was time to begin again at the other end.

He came upon Mr. Moonbeam turning a giant

grinding wheel; Nick Debrett held his saber to it, and showers of sparks flew into the air.

He was now at the deserted aft end of the ship, all the activity being concentrated forward. A glint of white caught his eye, and he looked up and shook his head disbelievingly. For a moment it seemed as though he had seen a naked woman diving from the *Blarney Cock*'s rail. Then he spied the heap of clothes—Jane Barnet's clothes—at the base of the rail, and looked over the stern. And there she was, graceful and bare as any fish, swimming toward the Three Sisters—the giant black rocks, each with its own sea-formed caves and tunnels, that rose from the sea near the ship's anchorage.

Nick Debrett's face was somber as he watched Ned Lynch watching Jane. It grew positively gloomy when he saw Lynch lowering one of the ship's dinghies to the water, with himself in it. Then he shrugged. A friend had to give advice, when he saw how things were going; but when it came down to it, advice and all the warnings in the world never changed anything. What would happen, happened; and all you could do was play the cards as they were dealt. Jane Barnet was definitely in the hand now; all he could hope was that she was not the queen of spades, the death card.

Jane had expected the sea cave to be dark, but the low sun cast warm light directly into it, and reflections from the smooth water outside rippled on its walls and vaulted ceiling; the whole interior was bathed in soft, shimmering light. It was as though she were swimming in the inside of a living jewel. She floated in the water, savoring its gentle touch; it relaxed her, soaking out the hates and tensions she had lived with these past two days. It had been foolhardy, she knew, to give in to the sudden impulse to strip and plunge into the sea, but after the planning session with Ned Lynch and Nick Debrett in Lynch's cabin, setting out how he and his men would handle the evening's raid on Durant's treasure, she had felt so tightly strung that she had needed the release.

She stiffened. A man's voice was coming from somewhere, from outside the cave, singing gently—a voice she recognized. She waited for the familiar surge of anger that anything to do with Ned Lynch aroused. But it did not come. Without being sure why, she swam for the cave entrance.

Ned Lynch, seated in the small boat, saw her dark hair glistening and the white glimmer of her body in the water as she emerged. He went on singing:

"As I walked out in Galway city
About the hour of twelve at night,
Who should I see but a fair young maiden
Washing her hair by candlelight?"

Jane swam slowly, lazily, listening, and was lost to sight in another sea tunnel.

"Wish I was a red rosy bush
On the banks of the sea;
Every time my true love did pass
She would pick a rose off me."

He rowed the boat slowly, not following her, but matching her movements; as if in a slow aquatic dance, they moved in and out among the rocks.

"Wish I lived in a lonely hollow
Where the sun don't ever shine.
If your heart belongs to another,
Then it cannot ever be mine."

Jane emerged from the last of the sea tunnels; Ned Lynch drew the dinghy alongside her. Treading water, she was aware of her nakedness but unconcerned; the sea clothed her enough for now, and Ned Lynch was somehow no longer the swaggering brute she had known and loathed; there was sadness, tenderness, and gentle humor in his singing—and something more, something that she realized was striking an answering chord in her.

"Wish I had a golden box
To keep my true love in.
I'd take her out and I'd kiss her twice,
Then I'd put her back again."

His voice died away, and Jane looked up at him gravely. "What do you want?"

He regarded her with frank admiration, but also with an air of detachment. After a moment, he leaned over the gunwale of the dinghy, bringing his face close to hers. She did not move away, and was aware that her heart was beating faster. Each searched the other's face as if memorizing every feature. Then Ned Lynch smiled slowly, reached into the bottom of the boat, and held up the bundle of clothing Jane had left behind on the *Blarney Cock*. "It's not impossible for a lass to get *off* a ship and not be seen—but getting on may be another matter."

Jane's face hardened. It was clear that he had no intention of turning his back while she scrambled into the dinghy and dressed. Typical of Ned Lynch to take advantage . . . The angry thought trailed off, and she realized that she had not truly felt it. And what she did feel was . . .

A smile—confident, welcoming, accepting—curved her lips, and she raised her arms from the water. Ned Lynch took her hands and gently drew her aboard. She seemed to rise from the sea like a statue formed of the foam, gently and unresistingly, still smiling and never taking her eyes from his.

Neither of them spoke, but neither of them doubted or questioned what was to happen, and it unfolded for them like a drama in which their roles had been preordained.

Later, Jane remembered one instant of dreamlike clarity: high in the darkening sky, a sea bird, its long wings reddened by the western sun, gave one sharp call that seemed an echo of her own cry at the moment when all the strength and warmth she had ever felt seemed to fuse and flower in her.

She was aware that the air was cooler now, the sun

almost set. Still not speaking, still not needing to, she and Ned unhurriedly dressed. Ned finally broke the silence. Jerking a thumb at the full moon rising in the east, he said, "Timc to be starting. When that's overhead, we'll be helping ourselves to Durant's treasure."

Jane nodded. What they had shared was supremely lovely, but it had not altered the fact that she had parents to rescue . . . and an enemy to kill.

Chapter 12

Clouds drifted past the moon, sending moving shadows along the deck and railing of H.M.S. *Forthright,* a middle-sized navy supply ship anchored in a cove some distance from Kingston.

It was the location of their anchorage that was vexing one of the sailors idling on deck. "It's hard, that's what it is," he grumbled. "We've got our cargo loaded, ready to sail for England at dawn. By rights, we should be treating ourselves to a last night ashore, not diddling around out in nowhere. What's it all about, anyway?"

"Governor's orders," another seaman said. "A special shipment to be loaded here. Don't make sense he couldn't do it right at the docks, but from what I hear, you don't ask the Governor questions, just do what he says and hope he likes the way you did it."

The shadow of the drifting clouds gave a constant effect of uneasy motion to the deck, and masked whatever hint there might have been of betraying movement, as hands grasped the rail at the deserted aftersection of the ship. Moving like shadows among the shadows, Ned Lynch, Debrett, and their crew slipped aboard, with Jane Barnet staying close to Ned. All were armed with their preferred weapons, most favoring the combination of cutlass and belaying pin. Mr. Moonbeam hefted a stout, gnarled club that he had bored down the center and filled with lead; Jane carried inside her blouse the dagger that had nearly emasculated Major Folly.

Obeying Ned Lynch's hand signals, half the pirates moved off behind Nick Debrett; the rest, and Jane, remaining with him.

Debrett's men waited on deck as he silently climbed the shrouds, moving up with the grace of a panther toward the crow's nest and its unaware lookout. Just below the platform, Debrett halted, removed a piece of cloth from his pocket, and folded it into a ball.

A final step upward brought him to the crow's nest. Before the startled lookout could react, Debrett pulled his legs out from under him, dumping him to the platform, and quickly stuffed the cloth into his mouth. The lookout's eyes bulged in sudden terror as he was lifted and casually tossed out of the crow's nest, and felt the rush of air as he plummeted toward the deck fifty feet below.

Debrett's men caught him in a stretched tarpaulin—one of them clubbing him briskly on the head with a belaying pin—rolled him up in it, and stowed him neatly against the rail.

At the beakhead, a crouching sailor complained bitterly, "That's the last time you'll find me eating Jamaican oysters. Me bowels are killing me right and proper." He let out an anguished groan.

Another seaman, lounging against the bow rail, shook his head. "If I've told you once, I've told you a hundred times: you've got to change your eating habits." He shook his head as a variety of sounds from the beakhead confirmed his diagnosis. "A man will live only as long as his belly will."

"Aye, mate, that's a fact." The sailor whirled, to confront Ned Lynch, and was instantly clubbed unconscious by Polonski and two other pirates. A brief startled squawk from the beakhead marked the taking-out of the incautious oyster fancier.

Polonski wagged his head. "My heart went out to dat one."

There were only three sailors left on deck now. They were still unaware of anything amiss, so stealthily had the pirates gone about their work. They learned quickly—and briefly—of the changed situation when a noose snaked about each one's neck and they were drawn up from the deck, legs twitching. Mr. Moonbeam and two companions, balanced on a spar above, tugged until the twitching stopped.

In a narrow passage belowdecks, Ned and Jane, followed by half a dozen of the *Blarney Cock*'s men, made their way quietly toward the galley. Just before they reached it, Ned took Jane's arm and whispered urgently to her.

She shook her head indignantly. "I will not!" she whispered.

He grinned. "It's for the good of the cause, girl. Besides, that way, we can take the lads easier, without having to slit their throats—it's your Christian duty."

She returned his smile. "All right, then. But don't expect me to make a habit of it."

He whispered very softly, "There's only one thing I'd like you to make a habit of, girl, and you know what that is."

He patted her shoulder and directed his men down a side corridor, following them. Jane opened the galley door.

The five men eating, drinking, and playing cards did not at first register her presence; nor did the huge black cook who was muttering over a pot on the brick stove. Then one man looked up from his mug of tea and gaped.

Framed in the doorway was a woman—unheard of for a navy ship out of harbor. Even more startling, the woman's blouse was unbuttoned to the waist, revealing most of her bosom. The effect on the sailor, who had missed shore leave in Kingston, and was beginning to forget any precise details about how women looked, was electric. His strangled gulp of amazement swung the others in the room to look.

Jane said nothing, but gave them a sultry smile, copied from what she recalled of one of Nick Debrett's women.

The men in the room were silent and open-mouthed. Then one of them found his voice. "Well,

well, now . . . could this be part of Lord Durant's treasure?" He started to rise from his chair, and the smile on Jane's face slipped a little.

"Afraid not, mate," said Ned Lynch, stepping through the rear door of the galley. By the time the confused sailors could turn away from the spectacle of Jane, they were all neatly knocked out and laid on the floor. One of the pirates began to strip off the cook's clothes. Jane turned away and faced Ned.

He looked down at her gaping blouse and said softly, "Careful that you don't catch a chill, Miss Barnet." She glared at him, flushed, and quickly began fastening buttons. The pirates chuckled, but were careful to do so discreetly; they had a sense that Ned Lynch wouldn't take kindly to any ribaldry about this girl.

On the afterdeck, two of the *Forthright*'s seamen emerged from their bunkroom in the hold and looked toward the shore. "Wonder when this fancy shipment's coming?" one said.

The other shrugged. "Almost any time now, from what the captain said. What say we get summat from the galley, stoke up a little before we get to the heaving and loading?"

"We could, but . . . wait, here's the cook coming now; what's he want, d'you suppose?"

Both watched the tall black figure in the familiar white garb approach. It was not until the man was almost on them that they noticed he had only one eye; and before they could react to that, Nick Debrett reached out, and with seeming gentleness, brought their heads together. There was a crisp, hollow sound, and both seamen sank to the deck.

Below, the door of the captain's cabin burst inward, and Ned Lynch sprang in, sword ready for instant combat. He lowered it and chuckled quietly. The captain was slumped over a table, snoring loudly enough to indicate that he was safely asleep for a long while yet. Lynch studied the uniform the man wore, and made a quick estimate of his general build—yes, it should do. And there on the wig stand was the officer's formal white wig, with his dress sword and buckler draped over a nearby chair. Ned Lynch grinned and began unbuttoning his shirt.

"That's the last of them," Mr. Moonbeam called down as he dropped a naked sailor, unconscious and trussed as neatly as a fowl, into the hold.

"Aye, then we'll keep them safe for ye," one of the two pirates guarding the prisoners called up. He looked at the twenty or more men, all inert, all tied, and most of them stripped of their uniforms, which Ned Lynch's men were even now donning.

"What a way for navy men to be," he observed. "Naked as needles, poor lads—lucky they're asleep, or they'd be dreadful shamed about it."

"So they would." The second pirate looked at the unconscious sailors thoughtfully. "Makes you kind of wish we'd captured a ship crewed by women, don't it?"

Lord Durant noted with satisfaction that, even though it was nearly midnight, the *Forthright*'s crew were alertly lining the rails as his small convoy approached her. For once, everything seemed to be going right. The oarsmen were handling the three longboats efficiently, the escort party of a dozen soldiers was trim and well-disciplined; the five heavy chests that held the treasure he had looted from the island were carefully stowed, ready for their trip to England. It had been wise to keep Major Folly out of this operation; if he had been along, doubtless the very boats would have burst asunder, dropping the chests to the bottom of the sea. The man really had a touch for disaster, though perhaps last night's lesson would teach him prudence.

The army captain in the first longboat called up to the ship, "Throw down the ladders and the sling! Make ready for Lord Durant!"

The reply drifted down from the deck: "Aye, aye, sir!"

Four Jacob's ladders were swiftly lowered over the side, followed by a substantial cargo sling.

As Durant began to climb one ladder, a burly man in the uniform of a petty officer bawled importantly, in a strong Irish accent, "Send for the captain. Tell him Lord Durant is boarding!"

"Very good, sir!" came the eager reply. The spectacle of old Moonbeam and his shipmate playing at being navy men was too much for one pirate at the rail, who started to laugh; Polonski's huge hand covered his mouth, and most of his face, not gently.

In the shadows, Nick Debrett, still in his cook's uniform, and Jane, clad somewhat unconvincingly as the cabin boy, watched the first chest being lifted onto the deck, and Durant stepping on board from the ladder. Jane's fists clenched tightly, and she bared her teeth in a feral snarl. This fat slug of a man had ruined her family and imprisoned her father, and tonight he would pay for it!

The main hatchway opened, and Ned Lynch, resplendent in his borrowed uniform, emerged and saluted Lord Durant. "Captain Devonshire-Bayne, at your service, sir." Some of the pirates' faces wavered as they suppressed their reaction to Lynch's imitation of a navy officer's drawling arrogance.

"Yes, yes, of course," Durant said impatiently, darting glances about at the progress of the loading of his chests.

"It is an honor and a privilege having you aboard, sir. Would M'Lord care to partake of a small libation in the captain's cabin?"

"Perhaps later. My concern now is that my belongings safely find their way onto your ship and into your most secure compartment."

As that was what Ned intended to do, though the ship he had in mind was the *Blarney Cock* and not the *Forthright,* he had no compunction about agreeing heartily. "As you wish. I can assure you, sir, that I will treat your treasure . . . as if it were my own."

"How reassuring, Captain," Durant purred. "Provided, of course, that you remember that it is *not* your own."

Ned Lynch gave a perish-the-thought laugh.

"Lord Durant is not without a sense of humor, I see."

Durant favored him with a tight smile, then cast another look over the side to check on his chests. Ned took the opportunity for a quick glance to where Nick Debrett and Jane were concealed; when he looked back, he found Lord Durant staring at him intently. "Something wrong, Captain?"

"Sir?"

"I said, is something wrong?"

Trying to appear blandly unaware of any possible difficulty, Ned said, "I don't follow your meaning, sir."

Durant glared at him, wondering if this popinjay of a sailor was another such booby as Folly, and squinted past him into the darkness. He stiffened and motioned to two of the accompanying soldiers. His voice was sharp as he gave them their orders. "You two, inspect that area over there." He pointed toward where Debrett and Jane stood concealed.

"But, sir," Ned said, wondering feverishly on what grounds he could protest or halt the search.

Durant turned to him and brought his face close. "It *distresses* me, Captain, to think that someone lurks in the shadows of your ship like a gray rat. You men, go now! Bring back any man you find there!"

Ned Lynch darted a look at the soldiers moving off on their mission. "I can *assure* you, Lord Durant, that you have no reason for concern."

The smile Durant gave him was mirthless, dangerous. "Let us just say that I have a suspicious nature, Captain; and up to this point at least it has served me well."

Ned nodded reluctant agreement. He turned toward the rail and called to the loading crew, "Hurry up with that cargo! *We haven't got all night!*" He hoped the extra urgency in the last sentence would go unnoticed by Lord Durant but not by his own men.

"Aye, aye, Captain," a voice floated up from below.

The two soldiers picked their way nervously among the tangle of ropes and the litter of strange maritime implements and protuberances that made the deck an obstacle course, especially in darkness. They were clearly visible to Jane and Nick Debrett, who stepped back quietly as they approached, until they were beside Mr. Moonbeam; the Irishman smiled and nodded his readiness.

"Well?" Durant called to the soldiers.

"Nothing, sir. We find nothing."

"As you see, Lord Durant," Ned Lynch said, hiding his relief, "there was no reason for—"

Durant ignored him. "Then look again!"

"Yes, sir."

Lynch looked past Durant and said heartily, "Ah! *Here* they are."

Lord Durant turned and saw with satisfaction the last of his chests coming over the side in the cargo sling. While his attention was occupied, Nick Debrett and Mr. Moonbeam silently sprang on the searching soldiers, clamped hands over their mouths, and hustled them away; Jane followed, plucking the victims' swords from their scabbards.

Ned sensed the flurry in the shadows and tensed briefly, then relaxed. No outcry meant that his people had prevailed. He addressed Durant unctuously. "Will My Lord allow me to show him the compartment I have selected for the purpose of storing his treasure?" The genuine enthusiasm in his voice might have been that of a shipmaster anxious to demonstrate his up-to-date facilities, or that of a pirate captain proposing to lure the man he had contracted to kill to a secluded spot.

"Yes, we'd best attend to that right now." Durant turned to the soldiers near him. "Guard the chests. No man is to touch any one of them until I return."

"Yes, sir," the nearest soldier said.

Lynch took Durant by the elbow. "Right this way, Lord Durant." He began to lead the acting royal governor toward the hatchway.

Durant stopped and shook off the guiding hand. "Where are the two men who went off?"

"Sir?" Lynch said, striving to look stupid.

"The two men I ordered to search? Where have they gone?"

"Ah . . . which two were those, sir?"

Durant's eyes narrowed. "What the devil is going on here, Captain?"

"Begging your pardon, sir, but—"

"But nothing! I am beginning to think you run a remarkably slovenly ship, sir!"

"I can assure you, sir, that—"

"Damn your assurances!" Durant's voice was rising and growing shriller in a way that those who knew him would have recognized and shuddered at. "I want to see the two men I ordered to search the starboard bow!"

Lynch cursed inwardly. Just at the moment of success, it was all starting to go wrong. And whatever was he to tell this Durant? The best he could come up with sounded feeble, even to him: "Well, they couldn't have gone *far,* sir."

Durant was nearly spitting as he thrust his face, suspicion written full on it, close to Lynch's. "Then . . . *where are they?"*

From behind the forecastle a slight figure darted, light glinting from the blade it held extended. Jane's voice throbbed with hatred as she shouted, "Gone . . . as you will be!" Her sword was a shining streak as it thrust toward Durant with a force no parry could deflect.

It would have been hard to find anybody who actually liked Lord Durant, but the speed of thought and reflex he now demonstrated was, in it's own way, admirable. Sidestepping Jane's lunge, he grabbed a bewildered soldier standing next to him and thrust him in her sword's path. The luckless soldier made not a sound as he fell back, eyes staring and the weapon's hilt protruding from his chest.

Before the corpse hit the deck, Ned Lynch had clubbed the army officer nearest him with the hilt of the captain's dress sword; snatched the officer's more battle-useful one from him; shed his stifling uniform jacket, wig, and tricorne hat; and begun a slashing attack at the closest body of soldiers.

There was a sound like a hundred knives being whetted as the pirates, led by Nick Debrett, drew their swords; Lord Durant's was out of its scabbard as quickly as theirs. He shouted, "Attack them! We've been tricked! Attack and kill them all!"

The sudden assault on Durant had not been seen clearly enough by the soldiers to allow them to make sense of his shrill cry for a general massacre of what, so far as they were concerned, was the crew of a ship of the Royal Navy, and confusion and indecision reigned among them for just long enough to lose them whatever advantage their military training might have given. By the time they collected themselves, they were a disorganized mob fighting for their lives as individuals, no longer a disciplined unit.

Lord Durant saw that the pirates' surprise attack was apparently winning the day, and again showed his speed of thought and action in a crisis by springing for the rigging and climbing swiftly up it. Ned Lynch witnessed his flight and began himself climbing in pursuit.

The fight was to the pirates' taste—harsh, brawling combat with no worry about tactics and formations. Mr. Moonbeam and Polonski moved through the startled redcoats like harvesters in the fields, Moonbeam wielding a discarded musket as a very effective club, Polonski chopping and cutting with a saber. At the edge of the deck, a pirate and a soldier, locked in a struggle that combined wrestling with savage slashes of their swords, broke through the rail, plunged into the water, and sank below the surface, still locked in mortal conflict.

Nick Debrett, laughing with exultation, took on man after man, toyed with them in swordplay a moment, then, one by one, brushed their swords aside and tipped them into the sea.

Jane moved through the knots of struggling men, mostly avoiding them but once in a while jabbing the sword she held into a soldier who was too close to her.

In a momentarily deserted area, she paused and looked upward.

The deck lanterns cast little light to the top of the rigging, but what there was, combined with the fitful glow of the moon, showed her Ned and Durant balanced on the same spar, swords raised and facing each other.

Durant's darting thrust, delivered expertly, almost threw Ned Lynch off-balance; he recovered, and retaliated with a low, swooping slash that might have severed Durant's legs at the ankles if he had not stepped nimbly back. Each man was in his own way enjoying the scene: Ned for the glory, the fantastic and unusual danger of the duel's location—one misstep would send him to burst on the deck like one of the bananas Nick and Jane had tossed from the wagon—and the sheer joy of fighting against a swordsman of Durant's masterful caliber; Durant for the strange, bizarre quality of the duel, the feeling of a supreme exercise of his skill, the dancelike movements forced on him and his opponent by the need to keep balanced on the narrow spar.

On the deck below, Jane could appreciate none of this—not that she would have, even if she had been able to view the scene more closely. To her, fighting was a way of defending oneself or harming one's enemy; that men could find it important, even absorbing, for other reasons, she could not understand. The issue to her was simple—the man she loved was up there, in mortal danger from her enemy. She spied a musket dropped on the deck by an overcome soldier, reached for it, checked that it was loaded and primed, pulled the hammer to full cock, and aimed it toward the rigging, seeking a clear shot at Durant.

Her quarry, forced to the end of the spar by Lynch's flurry of thrusts, leaped to the next spar, supporting himself for an instant by the rigging, then regaining his balance; Lynch sprang lightly to follow him, and the fight resumed.

Jane ground her teeth. Where they were now, she could not bring the musket to bear on Durant, and at any moment he might run Ned through or cause him to topple to his death on the planks of the deck. She began to climb the rigging, clutching the musket. Below her, she noted as she ascended, the fighting seemed to be dying down, with the pirates mopping up the last few soldiers.

Finally she was near the top of the foremast, on a level with Durant and Ned Lynch, only a few feet away. She crouched in the lines, and raised the musket, holding it as steadily as she could.

When the two men were briefly separated, she saw exultantly that she had a clear shot at Durant, and without giving herself a chance to think, fired.

The result was spectacular.

The musket ball sang past Durant's head and shattered the main pulley block, through which several crucial lines ran. A full-rigged ship, in order to be able to respond quickly to the winds and execute changes of course at its captain's will, is necessarily a complex and interdependent mechanism, controlled by myriads of lines. Allowance must be made for any one, or several, of these breaking under stress, but it had not occurred to *Forthright*'s designers that a solid-oak pulley block would give way before inspection showed signs of wear and tear that would call for its replacement. When all the lines that ran through this one were suddenly released, all the tensions and stresses that held the ship's rigging in its delicate balance were canceled.

Suddenly released spars whipped like unstrung bows; a furled topsail unfolded like a theater curtain descending; an unfurled one flapped free as its lines loosened; others fell limply to the deck, covering startled pirates and the soldiers they had subdued.

In the whirling chaos aloft, Ned Lynch was flung from his spar, and barely managed to clutch a stable portion of the rigging after he had fallen halfway to the deck.

Lord Durant had been a touch quicker, and fallen on his spar at the first shock of movement, clutching it tightly.

Jane, already off-balance from the musket's recoil, was flung from her perch into the air; a rigging rope, whipping wildly, coiled around her foot and stopped her, saving her from crashing to the deck forty feet below, but leaving her dangling helplessly upside down.

When the unstrung rigging reached its new equilibrium and stopped moving, Durant was the first to see her. He leaped from his spar to a tangle of rigging just above her, clutched her supporting rope, and laid his sword against it.

He gave a fierce shout. "Lynch!"

Nick Debrett, about to finish off the last remnants of opposition on deck, looked up, as did the other combatants. By unspoken agreement, the fighting stopped; what was taking place aloft suddenly had become the key to victory or defeat for either side.

Ned Lynch glared across the space that separated him from Durant and Jane. Durant did not speak, but grinned mirthlessly and pressed his blade harder against the rope. His ultimatum was clear without words.

Lynch, face set and hard, slowly lowered his sword.

"No!" Nick Debrett called up in anguish. This was what came of getting women involved in their work; at the crucial moment, Ned was being rendered as helpless as though he were bound hand and foot. "We've got them licked, Ned! We can't quit now!" The *Blarney Cock*'s men looked uneasily from Debrett to their captain. If Debrett's protest came to outright disagreement, mutiny, there would be a swift—and hard—choice to make.

Though it was a moment of deadly danger for Lord Durant, there was much to relish in the mental torture he was inflicting on Lynch, and in the heady power of life and death he held over the girl dangling beneath him; he could almost smell their fear and futile rage like fine perfume. His voice was smooth, close to playful. "This rope tingles in my hand, Mr. Lynch. Say the word, and I will gladly cut it through!"

"You made a vow, Mr. Lynch," Jane called. "Kill Durant or be responsible for the murder of all your men!"

Mr. Moonbeam joined in. "Captain! We fought to win, not surrender!"

"The girl is right, Ned!" Debrett shouted. "Listen to her!"

"A gentleman," Durant purred, "knows when to use his sword and when to lay it down. Have you forgotten, Lynch, that is what you once were?"

"I'm not a gentleman, I'm an Irishman!" Lynch snarled.

"*Now,* Lynch! I want to know your answer now!" Durant lightly drew his sword across the rope; one strand, sliced through, sprang free.

"Then tell him, Ned!" Debrett called desperately. "Your choice is clear!"

Ned Lynch stood in the rigging, aware, as if their gazes were solid matter pressing on him, of the eyes of his men, of Jane, of Durant, fixed on him. He gave a deep sigh; his fingers slowly opened, and his sword fell to the deck.

It clattered near Debrett, who looked at it lying there and murmured hopelessly, "My God . . ."

Durant nodded in satisfaction. "And the others, Mr. Lynch?"

Ned looked down to the upturned faces of his men and spoke with a painful effort. "Lay down your weapons, lads."

For a moment, everything seemed frozen to stillness on the ship. The pirates stood immobile, as did the few soldiers still on their feet; the only movement was Jane's slow, pendulumlike oscillation at the end of the rope.

Mr. Moonbeam was the first to break the spell. With a wordless exclamation of disgust he threw his gnarled club to the deck. The others of the *Blarney Cock*'s men grumbled and did the same; they stood surrounded by their abandoned weapons like strange trees growing in a field of steel.

One man only did not disarm himself. Durant

saw him and called, "You! Your sword! Lower it, you one-eyed ape!"

Nick Debrett stared up at Lord Durant, then looked toward Ned Lynch. Seven years of sailing and fighting together had taught them to read each other's faces without the need for words, and Lynch caught Debrett's message as easily as if it had been spoken: I'm taking action. Be prepared.

Debrett bawled up his defiance to Durant: "In a pig's eye, swine!" Then, swift and deadly as a black whirlwind, he turned on the three soldiers hemming him in, ran two of them through, kicked the third in the groin, darted past them, and leaped over the side of the ship.

Durant, in a frenzy, gestured with his sword to the soldiers. "Stop them!"

The troops moved to capture the pirates. Two of them grabbed Mr. Moonbeam's arms and wrenched them behind his back. Two more made for Polonski, who roared his rage and rammed them with his head; the force of his attack carried all three to the railing and through it. A splash and a pungent Polish curse marked their meeting with the sea.

In the general struggle now on, several more pirates dived over the side; others were subdued by Durant's soldiers. Durant himself scrambled down from the rigging to take charge, screaming, "Get them! Shoot them!" Muskets rattled at the railing as the soldiers fired vainly at the swimming pirates.

Ned Lynch slid his dagger from its sheath and called to his struggling men below, "Catch her!" He sprang to a spar near the rope from which Jane hung and slashed it through. She dropped like a stone and was caught by four pirates; then she and they were overwhelmed by a rush of soldiers.

Durant keened his rage as he saw Jane's release from her peril and Ned Lynch's next move, to the edge of the spar. "Stop him!"

Lynch dived from the spar, arrowing down to the water in a dive that took him well clear of the *Forthright*'s rail.

"Damn you all for fools! Shoot him! Kill him!" Spittle sprayed from Durant's mouth, and his eyes were staring wildly as he joined the soldiers at the railing.

There was no target for their muskets. Ned Lynch did not surface.

Durant whirled, incoherent obscenities bubbling on his lips. Through his rage, however, there was a scarlet thread of satisfaction. His treasure was safe, and even though Lynch and some of his rabble had escaped him, he had the rest . . . and Jane Barnet. They would afford him ample amusement before he was done with them; he would see to that.

A cold glimmer of light in the east revealed the shape of the *Blarney Cock* to the exhausted swimmers. Nick Debrett grasped the rope dangling over the side and helped the pitifully few others out of the water and on their way up it. There were no more than six of them. Polonski, beginning his climb, said mournfully, "They got Moonbim, damn shame. Good man, good heart."

"And the captain," Debrett said grimly.

Polonski looked over his shoulder. "Maybe not. Unless that's a porpoise?"

Debrett looked in the direction of Polonski's glance and saw a head moving toward them through the waves—Red Ned himself, by God!

A wavering cheer came from the pirates on the deck as they recognized Lynch. Debrett waited for him in the water, relief mingling with the bitterness he felt at what had happened on the *Forthright*—which amounted, in fact, to the destruction of the best pirate crew in the Indies, and not even in a fair fight, but through the captain's infatuation with a woman. He put that aside and said simply, "Glad you made it."

Lynch grasped the rope and gave a weak grin. "Damned near didn't. Had to swim underwater until I was out of the lobsterbacks' range. Could be that His Lordship thinks me drowned, which could be useful. . . ."

Debrett gave him a grim look. "Useful how?"

Ned Lynch did not reply directly, but looked toward the Jamaica shoreline, more visible in the dawn light with each moment. "If Durant has his way," he said musingly, "and he will, because there's no one to stop him, they'll all be hanged. All of them, Nick—Jane Barnet, her father, our lads . . . all of them."

"We're pirates, Ned. Not revolutionaries."

"But free men." Lynch stared hard at his friend. "So the choice is ours, isn't it?"

Chapter 13

Who first passed the word could never be said, but it was always true that anything happening in any part of Kingston was soon known in the market-place. Before the first soldiers appeared, the normal daily activity had dwindled, and the crowd was standing expectantly, the stilt walker Matthias, and James, his monkey, taking advantage of their elevation for a better view. The street acrobats were still for once; even the beggars abandoned their professional wheedling and stood mutely.

The throng stirred, and an uneasy mutter arose as the first mounted soldiers appeared at the edge of the market square. Then came a file of marching troops escorting a tattered throng of pirates, many showing fresh wounds, and one glaring, defiant girl.

To Jane, the Kingston crowd, alien and threatening only a few days before when she had been thrust among them, now seemed familiar and human compared to the impersonally efficient soldiers who surrounded her and to the loathsome creature who commanded them. She raised her head and marched proudly, as if on parade.

The captured pirates took heart and followed her lead; they entered the square with the air of conquerors, not prisoners.

The officer in charge of the detachment took the first cheer from the crowd as being one of appreciation for his men's work in capturing these public enemies;

but the growing swell of roars made it clear that encouragement was being offered to the pirates, not the soldiers.

As the noise increased, the horses stepped uneasily, laying their ears back, rolling their eyes, and whickering; one soldier was nearly pitched from his nervous mount.

"The *Blarney Cock* forever!" "Be of good cheer, lads!" "Dirty redcoats!" "Up with Lord Durant—to the gibbet!" The cries of the crowd alarmed the soldiers, and some drew sabers and glared menacingly.

The officer was sweating with anger and fear, then cursed as he reined his horse to a stop in front of the huge black man with a dozen knives strapped to his chest who stepped into his path.

"Stand aside for the King's army!" the officer shouted.

"*Ar*my?" Cudjo drawled. "I see no King's *ar*my. Monkeys, perhaps. Buffoons, possibly. Toads, ah, for sure. But an *ar*my? No, it could not possibly be!"

The crowd's laughter was perhaps less menacing than its jeers of a moment before, but even more infuriating to the officer. He drew his sword and yelled, "Stand aside or lose your head! Fair warning has been given!"

He held the blade poised for a downward slash, waiting for another defiant word or a move of those giant hands toward the glittering knives arrayed across the broad chest.

Cudjo Quarrel was still for a moment, then threw back his head and laughed; the buildings and walls of the marketplace echoed and amplified the full-throated sound.

The officer cursed again and spurred his horse forward. Followed by the taunts of the townsmen, the soldiers pushed their way through the square, hustling their captives toward the grim massiveness of the fortress ahead.

When they had left, the marketplace was abuzz with Kingstonians discussing the incident. Only Cudjo Quarrel was still, looking after the soldiers and prisoners. He was no longer laughing, and those who caught sight of his expression were very careful to step around him and not attract his notice.

Torchlight on the parapets of the fortress cast a dancing glow and deep shadow on the pavement near the gate. On its landward side, it presented a manmade cliff of stone to the town, as though a glacier had pushed into the streets and then been miraculously petrified.

In general, the fortress area was shunned by the townspeople as much as possible. It was not that there was any actual danger in walking close to it, but the huge building was a reminder of the arbitrary authority under which they lived and suffered. There had been a time when it had been a symbol of defense against a sea-borne enemy, and Kingston had gloried in the power of its great guns to hold off any invading fleet; but now its impregnable power was used against another enemy, more feared by Lord Durant than any foreigners —the people of Kingston themselves.

In spite of this, there was one hour of the day when some Kingstonians approached the fortress willingly. It had become a tradition for the street performers to put on a show once a night before the main gate; the tumblers and acrobats would nightly gyrate, the stilt walker would go through his elevated—in height only, not in tone—capers with the help of his monkey, the balladeer would sing songs of notable bawdry (some, though he did not know it, derived from verses Ned Lynch and Nick Debrett had improvised, which had later traveled through the waterfront haunts), the very beggars would raise their wheedling and whining to a level of art. The bored soldiers on guard duty looked forward to this established interlude in their routine, and rewarded their entertainers with at least a few coins—and if some poor wretches rotting in Durant's dungeons were heartened by a brief reminder that life as they had known it still went on beyond the fortress's dank walls, so much the better.

This night, at the customary hour, the stilt walker, the acrobats, and the others began to drift toward the fortress. There was an unaccustomed purpose in their approach, although it would not have been evident to a watcher . . . and they were not alone. Out of the malodorous alleys of the slums, from beneath the market stalls where they made their homes, from hovel and tavern, the poor, the wretched, and the dispossessed of Kingston joined them.

In the fortress, all was much as usual. The off-duty soldiers lounged in the barnlike stone barracks area; the officer in charge of the fortress for the night had, after assuring himself at ten o'clock that all was well, with all prisoners and guards where they should be, retired to bed. Major Folly had hoped to get some useful reading in before falling asleep, but the treatise on the rules and regulations for military executions, though containing much new information for him, had soon proved as effective as a sleeping draft. His slumber was deep but occasionally troubled; the ointment Durant's slaves had placed on his wounds was remarkably effective, but the healing scars still ached with every movement, and even a deep breath gave him a twinge that would make him twitch and mutter in his sleep.

Walking his patrol on the parapets, one guard greeted a stationary comrade. "How's the little woman?"

"Still alive, curse my luck."

The first guard looked past the huge main gate with its eight guards, and saw the entertainers approaching. He squinted; somehow there seemed to be more of them than usual. Maybe it would be an especially interesting show. . . .

"Your friends are back," he said.

The other man sighed and took some coins from his pocket. "They'll break me yet." He tossed the money down to the street, and the ragged entertainers scrambled for them—perhaps not with their usual avid concentration.

"You needn't keep encouraging them, you know."

The second guard shrugged. "What else am I to do up here, night after night? Besides, I get more pleasure from them than I do at home!"

The first guard nodded sympathetically and continued his patrol back to his own post. The man he had left looked down at the street entertainers preparing their acts. As usual, the tumblers were first. Tonight they had brought a portable seesaw with them. Setting it to one side, they practiced vaulting over each other, doing somersaults in the air and landing on each other's shoulders. The guard yawned; it was skilled work, that, to be sure, but he'd seen the same thing practically every night he'd been on duty at the fortress. He looked at his pocket watch; time to walk his stretch of wall and check in with the sentry on the next post.

As he trudged away, the tumblers turned to the seesaw. One stood on the lower edge of the board; another climbed on his shoulders; then, when the sentry was out of sight, he jumped to the upper end, catapulting his partner upward. He did not come down. In a moment, the people in the street saw him wave cautiously from the parapets.

Farther down the wall, at a well-shadowed part of it, Cudjo Quarrel, using the tough vines that were slowly strangling an old tree nearby, slid up as silently and smoothly as a snake. Two feet from the top, he stopped and held himself as motionless as a shadow; a sentry was walking slowly by, just above him. With one hand, Cudjo caught the soldier's ankle, plucked him from his beat, and hurled him to the street below. Two men appeared from the darkness and dragged the fallen man away. Cudjo looked down and grinned, then hoisted himself up to the parapet and loped down it, keeping to the shadows.

The bored guard who had thrown coins to the entertainers was returning to his original post, mildly interested to see if the tumblers might by chance have added anything to their usual routines. It seemed to him, as he approached, that there were fewer of them than before, one less at least; where could the other man be? His unspoken question was answered by a sudden shove in the small of his back; the man who had been catapulted onto the parapet pushed him neatly into the waiting arms of the performers below.

Carefully keeping out of sight of the remaining

sentries and the guards on duty at the main gate, the street people of Kingston surrounded the fortress. One group of them, led by Ned Lynch, Nick Debrett, Polonski, and the other uncaptured men of the *Blarney Cock*, came to where Cudjo Quarrel was waiting on the walls above. They tossed the ends of half a dozen ropes up to him; he quickly secured them around the crenellations of the parapet. The pirates and their allies quickly swarmed up them. Polonski thought to make his way up faster, using the vines and trees that had taken root in the ancient wall; but the first projecting tree he tried came away from the wall, sending him sprawling. A shipmate tossed him a rope; he tested its strength carefully before undertaking the climb.

The tumblers, now unobserved from above, formed a human pyramid with practiced speed, the topmost man's shoulders coming to just below the parapet; a dozen street people appeared from the darkness and clawed their way to the top of the wall.

The stilt walker, Matthias, strode up to the parapet on his longest stilts, turned, and sat on it, drawing them up with him; his monkey chose a route up a tree, then joined Matthias, looking about and chattering with animated interest.

At this point, without any of its garrison being aware of it, the walls that ran around the rambling old fortification were almost completely occupied by the pirates and the street people of Kingston. Only the guards on duty at the parapet above the main gate were as yet unmolested. These now looked down with interest and envy at the four soldiers stationed at the gate itself.

Though ladies of the night usually avoided this area, three of them had approached the gate, and were, with the accustomed gestures of their trade, announcing their availability; the soldiers at the gate were startled, pleased, and definitely interested; one began to jingle coins in his pocket in a meaningful manner. Though the guards on the parapet regretted their isolation, it was beginning to look as though they might at least have a good view of whatever action was to come, and they focused their attention below wholeheartedly.

Kingston had long outgrown the fortress, which had been constructed with a view to being used much as a medieval castle was, a place to which the entire population could resort in case of an enemy siege. Within thick walls so many buildings of different kinds had been erected that the place had once resembled a miniature city. Now most of them had fallen into ruin, the process hastened by the swift growth of trees whose roots pried apart the soft limestone of which the greater number had been constructed. Only the buildings in use—the barracks, officers' quarters, the officers' and men's messes the stables, armory and powder-storage room, and so on—were maintained; the others had been allowed to crumble and were no more than remnants of walls and archways. A gigantic banyan tree had established itself in one corner of the main wall, sending twisted roots snaking down the wall to the ground level of the huge interior courtyard.

The dim light from the barracks briefly revealed Cudjo Quarrel swiftly moving down one of these roots from the parapet. The few soldiers on guard—a duty which seemed pointless to them, for what could there be to guard against *inside* the fortress?—failed to see him.

Nor did they see the dead-silent human tide that seemed to flow down the walls—pirates and townspeople sliding, jumping, climbing to the courtyard—until it overwhelmed them, and under Ned Lynch's direction, stifled and rendered them unconscious.

A tug of a rope, a squeeze of a neck, a swift jab to a vital point—all effective methods, but complete silence could not be hoped for; some muffled cries and grunts escaped the soldiers before they fell.

The guards at the gate were marginally aware of a stir somewhere behind them, and turned to peer toward the interior of the fortress. The women engaging their attention heard it, too, and had been primed as to how to deal with it: one unobtrusively reached out and twitched a companion's low-cut blouse from one shoulder and burst into a shrill giggle. "Jenny, yer port light's showin'! Is t'other one green for starboard, I wonder?"

The eyes of all the soldiers at the gate and on the parapet above snapped back to the laughing whores and Jenny's partly exposed bosom, which she made no effort to cover. The sounds, if there had been sounds, from inside the fortress were forgotten.

Leaving the trussed soldiers behind, Ned Lynch led his motley band to the largest building within the walls, a huge edifice, now partly ruined, that had once been the island's hall of government. That function had long ago been transferred elsewhere, but reminders of the hall's busier days could be seen in the fragments of staircases that led to its various levels. Ned Lynch nodded grimly as he surveyed it, and waved his ragged army on; they swarmed up the walls to the partly fallen-in roof, took positions on the stairways, and some who knew the place best from bitter experience made their way to the subterranean entrances. This building was their main objective, for even in its decrepit state, Lord Durant had found use for it.

The guards at the gate were now totally absorbed with the women in front of them; it would have taken far more than the clink of a dislodged stone and the rustling of a multitude on the move to distract them. One guard was helping Jenny readjust her blouse; but he must have been unused to the vagaries of women's clothing, for it slipped from her other shoulder. The guards on the parapet leaned over for the best view.

From a corner of the roof where part of it had fallen in, Ned Lynch looked into the vast interior of the building. His face was savage. He had known, in a general way, what Durant was up to, but it had been none of his business. But to see it made a difference.

Chained prisoners, filthy and sagging in their manacles, lined the walls; others were secured to the giant pillars that rose to the roof. Wooden stocks—clamping head, hands, and feet rigidly—held some, including, Lynch noted, Mr. Moonbeam.

There was horror enough to be seen at the floor

level; what was above it was worse, an example of Lord Durant's playful taste for the grotesque. Eight large cages, constructed of riveted metals bars and bands, hung on chains from the rafters, dangling six feet above the floor; a giant might have used them to house a parrot or a canary built to his own scale. But these held Lord Durant's "pets," the prisoners singled out for special treatment.

A raised platform in the center of the floor held a table and some cots for the use of the twenty soldiers guarding the prisoners; these were now sleeping or playing chess or cards, unaware of the stirring in the shadows as Ned Lynch's men took their positions.

At the wave of his hand, there was a silent rush; from the partly open roof, from windows and doors, up from the very ground, pirates and street people surged toward the guards.

The surprise was complete, but the soldiers reacted swiftly, some grabbing weapons, others shaking their sleeping fellows awake; one rang an alarm bell to summon aid.

As the battle was joined in the prison compound, Lynch, flanked by Nick Debrett and Cudjo Quarrel, appraised the situation briefly; Lynch nodded a signal.

Debrett jumped from the rafters, breaking his fall on one of the hanging cages, swung from it to the floor, and charged the platform with drawn sword.

From his perch on the rafters, Cudjo Quarrel, like a black god of lightning, hurled the thunderbolts of his knives down at the rallying soldiers; like tenpins, his targets went down as they ran to join the fight. Cudjo's hands moved so quickly that within five seconds only one dagger remained of his dozen, held back for hand-to-hand fighting. Ned Lynch blinked, and briefly thought that if there could be a gun made that fired that fast, it would make fighting a sorry business indeed.

Ned drew his sword; he and Cudjo Quarrel gave simultaneous war cries—one handed down from the warriors of ancient Ireland, the other from the spearmen of the kings of Benin—and slid down the chains supporting the cages and into the battle on the floor.

To the stupefied prisoners it seemed as though legions of imps and devils had come to attack their oppressors: a man on stilts strode among the combatants, striking at the tops of the soldiers' heads with a club, and when he was overset, used his stilts like twin flails; a chattering monkey perched on a redcoat's shoulder and clawed the man's face until he yelled and dropped his sword; men in bright clothes arced through the air like human cannonballs, felling their opponents; two giant black men struck and slew with the roaring delight of demons. But in the middle of it all, there was one familiar face, aglow with a savage joy.

"It's Ned Lynch!" one prisoner quavered. "Ned and Nick Debrett!" There was a hoarse, barely human cheer from the chained captives.

Jostled by the combatants, the huge cages began to swing in wild arcs; the prisoners inside them, once the motion had started, urged it on by hurling themselves from side to side, trying to aim them at the guards.

Jane Barnet, swinging her cage like a maddened pendulum, smiled angrily as its edge caught a startled guard in the face and he disappeared. She was jolted to one side as the cage was slowed. She looked down, saw fingers holding it from below, and stamped.

"Ow, lass! Would you flatten my fingers till they're no use for anything but hair ribbons?"

"Oh . . . sorry, Ned."

Lynch, hanging from the swaying cage, motioned to Nick Debrett, who ended his duel with two guards by one devastating slash, removed a key ring from one body, and tossed it to him.

Lynch scooped the flying keys from the air, unlocked the cage door, pulled Jane from inside, and held her in one arm. At the top of its arc, he released his grip on the cage, and they soared to the platform, landing on one of the cots. It collapsed under the impact, folding around them and leaving them entwined. For a moment they stayed there, holding each other tightly, ignoring the clash and cry of the bizarre battle around them.

Nick Debrett dodged a concerted sweep of three

sabers by falling under it, and found his face pressed almost against Lynch's and Jane's.

"We've come to make war, Captain," he said softly, "not love."

The man and the woman grinned sheepishly as Debrett sprang away and into battle. Ned untangled himself from the cot and from Jane, rose, and drew his sword, looking for the next opponent; a ravingly angry soldier ran toward him and engaged him.

Jane called out, "My father!"

"Where is he?" Lynch sized up the man fighting him—he'd be ripe for the sidestep-and-cut-from-the-left about now. . . .

"In the catacombs!"

Step, then chop! Ah, yes, that usually did it. He left his fallen foe rolling on the floor, took Jane by the hand, and ran with her through the melee toward an archway. He signaled Nick Debrett to accompany them.

Polonski was overjoyed to find Mr. Moonbeam, and was busily trying to free him from the giant beam that pinioned his neck and limbs. The table leg he was using as a pry bar snapped. "Sorry, Moonbim. Minute . . ."

He grabbed the two pieces of the stock, the hinged top and the solid base, and wrenched them in opposite directions. His enormous shoulders bulged, and his stolid face reddened; every part of his body seemed to strain with the effort. Finally the wood gave way with a rending sound, and Polonski fell to his knees, panting.

Mr. Moonbeam, surveying the raging fighting with a professional eye, stretched his stiffened arms and legs, then bent to help his friend.

Three soldiers, spying two pirates at a disadvantage, rushed at them with swords ready to strike. Polonski saw them, roared, lowered his massive head, and dived for them without rising from his knees. All three fell, having suffered close to a dozen broken ribs among them.

The stone floor of the ruined hall was so thick that the sounds of fighting above soon died away as Ned Lynch, Nick Debrett, and Jane raced down a spiral staircase beneath it. The rocks beneath the fortress was honeycombed with passageways and cells once designed to serve as a last hiding place and a possible escape route for suvivors of a successful attack, now used by Lord Durant for darker purposes.

A barred iron gate stopped them at the foot of the stairs. Through it, between them and the maze of corridors that flickering torches on the walls revealed dimly, a guard sat asleep on a stool.

Ned Lynch gestured to Jane and Debrett to stay where they were, and ran back up the stairs. At the archway leading to the scene of the still-hot fight, he found Matthias, the stilt walker, jabbing his stilts among the combatants where they would do the most good. James, his monkey, was perched on his shoulder. Lynch attracted his attention and called quietly, "The apc! Quickly!"

Matthias nodded and gave one last thrust with his stilt. It passed between the legs of a soldier dueling with a pirate; the latter grabbed the end and hoisted upward. The soldier, suddenly and painfully lifted into the air, wailed and toppled sideways. Matthias abandoned the stilt and raced after Lynch.

At the gate, after Ned had hastily explained what was wanted, Matthias spoke briefly to his monkey and sent him through the bars. The animal scampered to the sleeping guard, lifted a half-empty bottle of rum from beside him, and chattered proudly.

The stilt walker shook his head severely and patted himself on the hip. The monkey scratched himself in the same spot, then gave a soft chirr of understanding and slid a heavy key ring from the guard's belt. He scampered back through the bars and handed the keys to Matthias, who passed them on to Ned Lynch.

The first key Lynch tried grated in the lock but did not turn it. He cursed softly and tried the next. This one worked; the gate creaked loudly as it opened. Lynch and Jane hurried past the guard, who had moved slightly in his sleep at the sound. Nick Debrett paused by him and rapped him smartly behind the ear with the hilt of his dagger; the sleeper relaxed into a slumber which should last for some hours, Debrett estimated. Nick turned to find the stilt walker apologetically holding out a handful of coins. "Yours, mister," he said apologetically as Debrett wonderingly took them. He turned to his simian colleague. "Bad monkey! Must learn when pick pockets, when *not.*"

He shrugged at Debrett's amused look, and both moved off down the corridor after Ned Lynch and Jane.

Off both sides of the low-ceilinged passage were cells. Some, huge and vaulted, perhaps once intended for the laudable purpose of storing casks of wine, held many prisoners; others were smaller, scarcely more than hollowed-out caves, each containing one wretch in solitary misery. As the four invaders passed, hands were held out to them through the barred doors, and pleas for food, water, and freedom came to their ears.

"In good time, in good time," Ned muttered, steeling himself to pass by these pitiable victims of Lord Durant. They finally found the cell they were looking for, the smallest and dankest of all, its gate scarcely three feet high.

Sir James Barnet, gaunt and beard-stubbled, peered out at them. When Ned Lynch opened the lock, Jane bent and crawled inside to embrace her father. He trembled in her arms and murmured, "Praise heaven you are safe!" She nodded and kissed him; bright tears stood in her eyes.

Ned Lynch helped them both out, he and Jane supporting Barnet as they moved back down the tunnel. Lynch tossed the key ring to Nick Debrett. "Tell them all to get out as fast as they can, Nick. It won't be healthy here in a while, you know."

Debrett nodded and passed the keys from one set of clutching, beseeching hands to another, letting them pause only long enough to unlock each cell door in turn. The corridor filled with amazed, overjoyed prisoners, who shambled and stumbled, under Nick Debrett's prodding, toward the exit.

At the main gate, the last guard, having been driven nearly out of his mind by watching his companions enjoy the three whores, was at last free to take his turn. At the sound of a galloping horse, he groaned and cursed, making desperate efforts to refasten his breeches buttons. He could not manage it, and held his coat closely around him as the horse reined to a stop.

"Halt! Who goes there?" he said feebly.

The rider spoke harshly. " 'Tis I, Willard Culverwell, Lord Durant's personal secretary. Have you no eyes in your wooden heads?"

The soldiers lowered their muskets, sickly certain that their pleasure was about to be paid for in more than clinking coin. "Beg pardon, sir," the challenger mumbled.

"So you had better! What the devil is going on here? Who are these women?"

"Women, sir?" The guard toyed with the idea of saying that his sisters had stopped to pass the time of day, but the three glassy-eyed women, faces swollen and hair disarrayed, skirts pushed up above the knees —and Jenny's blouse completely down to her waist— would not pass muster as visiting relatives.

"Whores, then! Is this a proper manner for a soldier to stand guard!" From long observation, Willard Culverwell was able to edge his voice with an imitation of Lord Durant's piercing menace, and the guards recognized the tone.

"No, sir. But, you see, sir, we were only—"

"Enough! Lord Durant will demand to know who is responsible for this outrage!"

"But, sir," the guard quavered. "We ourselves are in the dark. Never before did—"

"The dark? You shall all be in *chains* if I am not quickly satisfied! Now, open the gates so that I can speak with Major Folly. I am quite certain that he will have a few choice words to say about this!"

"Yes, sir." The guard looked behind him and shouted importantly, "Open the gates! Open the gates for Lord Durant's secretary!" The massive wooden doors began to part.

Inside the prison hall, the battle was over; former prisoners, pirates, and street people embraced each other joyfully; Nick Debrett and some of the *Blarney*

Cock's men were taking considerable satisfaction in locking the surviving guards in the cages, clamping them in the stocks, and chaining them to the wall.

Ned Lynch hoisted himself up to a cage, gave a polite smile to its gloomy new occupant, and climbed up its supporting chain to the rafters. James, the monkey, scampered up and joined him, chattering with excitement.

Lynch and the monkey looked down on the surging, elated crowd. He called down to them, "Lads and ladies! *We've won!*"

The full-throated cheer that burst from the crowd filled the vast room that had seen so much degradation and terror, and rang like a knell in the ears of the captured guards.

In the fortress's great stone barracks, it did not resound so loudly, but it was audible enough, and alarming enough, to rouse the sleeping soldiers and alert the few already awake. Responding to their training, they reached for weapons and ran for the barracks doors. Major Folly's corporal joined the rush, then stopped; the major would have his hide for certain if he wasn't told of this. And besides, who knew what sort of thing that devilish yell had betokened? Far better to let the major look into it.

The fortress gates were fully open now, and the guards heard the roar of sound clearly. Before they could take any action, they were alarmed to see Willard Culverwell, dismounted and inside, wave vigorously toward the street.

"Something's up . . . close the gates!" the guard in charge yelled. His men ran to do so, impeded by the three whores, who clung to them grimly. Before they could grasp the gates, a mass of men and women appeared from the shadows and rushed them; like chips in a river, they were dragged from their posts and carried along.

The first group of soldiers to emerge from the barracks tumbled down the building's front stairs, directly into the path of the oncoming crowd. One private leveled his musket; a sergeant struck it from his hands, muttering, "Don't be a fool! They'd rip you in a score of pieces if you loosed off a shot at them! We'll make off that way and try to form ranks."

But as the soldiers moved out of the crowd's way, they confronted a wave of released prisoners and their rescuers coming from the prison compound; they stopped helplessly in their tracks and waited for their fates.

In a small courtyard near the stables, Folly's corporal struggled with a high-spirited horse. The young major, eyes still puffy from sleep, pounded down the stairs from his quarters, buttoning his uniform coat, and grabbed the reins. "Quickly! Open the side gate!"

The corporal ran to a small gate in the nearby wall, tugged at the heavy sliding crossbar, and managed to wrestle it open. His heart sank as he saw crowds of townspeople outside, waving torches and singing. Whatever was up was bigger trouble than any he had ever seen.

Folly jumped onto the horse, was nearly pitched off, and then got the beast under control. He spurred it toward the gate and through it; the corporal had gotten halfway through saying "Good luck, sir" when he was knocked to the ground by the major's galloping exit. He had just regained his knees when the townspeople, seeing a new way in, poured through the passageway, engulfing him.

In the great courtyard, the scene might have been a huge fair rather than the field of a battle just concluded. And, strictly speaking, it had not even been a battle. Though a few soldiers had at first resisted, the crowd did not fight them, merely swarmed around them, taking their weapons, frustrating any attempts at maintaining a military formation, and finally absorbing them. Now that the troops were no threat, the Kingstonians felt no rancor toward them, and many were kissed, hugged, and dragged into the celebration. Where the press of the crowd was not too great, musicians broke out their instruments and launched into tunes that started dancing among those who had room to move.

Ned Lynch frowned and ran to the top of the barracks steps. He cupped his hands around his mouth and yelled at the crowd, repeating his message as it became evident that he could not be heard.

Those nearest him heard a few disconnected words: ". . . can't stay . . . any minute . . . get out . . ." One man who caught the fragmentary warning smiled and shook his head. That Lynch fellow was acting just like a tavern landlord warning about closing time. Maybe he was afraid they'd overstayed their welcome!

Lynch nearly groaned with impatience. Any second now, Culverwell would be doing his part, and then all hell would break out, with these dancing fools in the middle of it!

And it was precisely at that moment that Willard Culverwell, having made his way to a deserted tower on the ramparts, lifted his crossbow, ignited a fuse, and lofted a signal flare into the sky, out toward the sea.

The flash and bang of the flare attracted no notice from the revelers in the courtyard, but it shook the sentry at the execution dock, walking his rounds under the gallows, out of the trance his duty normally induced. "What in—"

That was as far as he got; a wet, muscular arm slid around his neck and squeezed until he slumped. The pirate, dripping from his swim ashore, dropped the sentry to the dock, then turned and waved seaward.

The *Blarney Cock*, crewed by only a handful of men, ghosted in under reefed sails and nestled gently and silently against the dock. The wet pirate vaulted on board and ran to join the gun captain in hauling a canvas cover from the squat mortar bolted to the deck. The gunner beckoned to the men coming down from the rigging after furling the sails. "Give us a hand, mates."

"Sails is me duty, not mortars," one complained.

"Death'll be your duty, mate, if ye disobey the orders of the senior officer left on board," the gun captain said reasonably.

All the pirates turned to and wrestled the mortar around, adjusting its elevation until the gunner was satisfied. He calculated the angle, inspected the bagged charge of powder and the hollow, fused ball it was to project, and said, "That'll just do, I think."

He dropped in the charge and the ball, lit the fuse with a slow match, then placed the match against the touch hole. A bang like the crack of doom seemed to split the eardrums of the pirates and a lurid flash lit them up sharply; the recoil drove the ship several feet deeper in the water and set it to rocking. Before the noise had died away, the gun captain was swabbing the smoldering mortar to cool it for the next shot.

Though Ned Lynch's calls for attention drew no response from the roistering crowd in the fortress, the boom of the mortar, followed by an explosion that destroyed one corner of the main wall, was wonderfully effective; they were silent in an instant.

"Friends," Lynch called. "Let's leave this place—before it buries us!"

The crowd gave a shout of agreement and began pouring toward the main gate; the soldiers mixed in with them showed no desire whatever to stay behind.

Mr. Moonbeam anxiously asked another pirate, "Have ye seen Polonski?" The pirate shook his head. "God in heaven," Moonbeam muttered. "Is the dear fellow to be left behind?" He reluctantly joined the surge toward the gate, looking behind him for a familiar face.

The twin reports of the mortar and its exploding projectile carried through Kingston and beyond, to where Major Folly was galloping on the highway; at the flash and noise, he spurred his horse harder.

The last of the mixed crowd of Kingstonians, pirates, captives, and soldiers was out of the gate and moving down the streets outside when the mortar lofted its second shot. The keenest eye might just have followed the trail of sparks from the fuse as the massive bomb rose in the air, slowed, and descended, crashing through the wooden roof of a large stone building. It landed on the flagged floor, feet away from casks of powder stacked to the ceiling. Its fuse hissed out its last fractions of an inch.

To the people in the street, the glare from the

fortress made it seem for an instant as if the sun had suddenly risen; there was a deep, thundering roar; the ground trembled as though in an earthquake.

They scurried to dodge falling fragments of rock and roof timbers, and sheltered behind walls and houses, many risking danger to watch the incredible spectacle.

As the explosion of one ammunition-storage chamber set off another, the gut-wrenching reports continued; the glow of one explosion had not time to fade before another took its place. One section of the main wall bulged, crumbled into its component stones, and slid into the street, revealing something of the hell inside. Like a volcano, the fortress was devouring itself, and filling the air with a pall of dust, smoke, and cinders.

Cheers from the watching crowd followed each stage of the hated fortification's destruction. Mr. Moonbeam did not join in them, but looked mournfully on. To the townsmen standing next to him, he said brokenly, "He was in there . . . my friend. He was really a very nice man. . . ."

The townsman had no idea what Mr. Moonbeam meant, but was willing to nod sympathetically.

"He was from one of them places east of the Germanies, poor fellow. Ah, 'twas a misfortunate day when he . . . uff!"

A pair of giant arms squeezed his waist, lifted him from the ground, and whirled him about. "Polonski! Ye made it!" Polonski nodded ecstatically.

The explosions continued, lighting the night sky. The crowd now began to form into a procession, with Ned Lynch, Nick Debrett, Jane Barnet and her father, Cudjo Quarrel, and Willard Culverwell in the forefront. Major Folly's corporal, dazed but somehow happy, trotted along with the rest of them.

Another lightninglike flash split the sky, followed by a heavy thump and a profound rumble. "Those dungeons will break no more bodies, mates!" Nick Debrett called.

"We've got one more task ahead, lads, and we'd

best get at it," Ned Lynch said soberly. He drew Sir James Barnet and Cudjo Quarrel aside and spoke to them; both nodded, and Quarrel led Sir James into the shadows.

The first trickle of excited spectators who had witnessed the end of the fortress were racing through the shabby street at the waterfront where the Barnet women had been lodged, shouting the news. They were obliged to dodge a farm wagon, driven at breakneck speed by a giant black, until it halted in front of the lodging house. Cudjo Quarrel leaped from the driver's seat and tried the front door. Finding it locked, he braced his feet and tugged on the handle. The door splintered away from its hinges; he tossed it to the street and returned to the wagon to assist Sir James Barnet from it. Barnet grasped Cudjo's arm for support as they moved to the open doorway. The landlady popped into it, looking, with her filthy robe and malignant face, like an overused Judy in a puppet show; she snarled at them, torn between rage and fright. "Here, now, what d'you think you're doing?"

Cudjo Quarrel reached out, placed his hand on her face, and pushed; she tumbled backward into her room and sprawled on the floor. "Improving the neighborhood, my sweet," he said with dangerous gentleness.

From only a few streets away, the triumphant roar of the crowd could be heard. Lady Barnet appeared at the top of the stairway and called down to Cudjo, "What is happening?"

Sir James was about to call out to her, but Cudjo motioned him to be silent and to step out of her line of sight. "A message from your daughter, Lady Barnet," he called up.

She ran down the stairs. "What is . . . ? *Oh!*" At the sight of her husband, she threw herself into his arms.

The embracing couple was the first sight seen by the main body of marchers celebrating their victory. First one recognized them, then others, and voices rang out: "Sir James Barnet!" "God bless Sir James!" "God save the King and the Lord Chief Justice!"

The crowd cheered when Sir James straightened, faced them, and waved his thanks. Then a voice called, "God save the *new* Governor—Sir James Barnet!"

Barnet seemed about to protest for an instant, but the cry was taken up by the throng; it became a chant, and before he could make any objection, if he had wished to, he was seized, raised above the crowd, and carried off in triumph.

Lady Barnet, happy but shaken, wiped a tear from her eye. Cudjo Quarrel's face bore a broad, happy grin. Jamaica would never be the same after this night, and he had had a strong hand in the change. Now, *there* was something to make a man feel what power was; it was well enough to be able to beat anyone in a fight, or to split a playing card with a thrown knife, but to topple a tyrant—that was something else. His grin grew broader: for a man with a new-found taste that way, it would never be hard to find something to do in the Indies.

Chapter 14

Major Folly vaulted from his horse in front of Lord Durant's mansion; three strides took him past the guards and through the ornately decorated front entrance; he bounded up the velvet-carpeted staircase four steps at a time.

In Durant's bathroom, the Acting Governor—unaware of being deposed at just this moment by popular acclaim—was at a favorite game. Submerged in his marble bath, he faced the vacant-eyed lute player who shared the tub with him. Each of them maneuvered a cleverly carved ship model on the perfumed water; Durant's was a completely detailed miniature of a British man-of-war, while the lute player had been given one looking remarkably like the *Blarney Cock*.

Lord Durant's enigmatic female companion sat on a cushion by the side of the sunken tub, trailing one hand in the water.

Durant signaled, and the two men guided their ships toward the center of the bath. The lute player made perfunctory attempts to keep his vessel out of the way of Durant's, but the battleship finally struck it amidships.

"Boom, boom," Durant said with satisfaction. The lute player burst into shrill laughter; the dark woman looked on expressionlessly.

The bathroom door burst open, and Major Folly rushed in, skidding on the slick marble floor and only just recovering his balance at the edge of the tub. He looked down at the men in it, and quickly looked up and across the room.

"What in the name of hell is meant by this outrage?" Lord Durant grasped the edge of the marble tub and seemed on the point of rising from it; Folly desperately hoped he wouldn't.

Still winded from his ride and the dash upstairs, he gasped, "The fortress. My Lord, the fortress!"

"Yes? Yes? Out with it, you blubbering fool!"

"Invaded, sir—we have been invaded!"

Durant relaxed his grip and sank back into the tub. "Invaded? By whom? Speak up!"

"Buccaneers, my Lord—pirates! Cutthroats! Red Ned Lynch and his men! And by the people. My Lord, the people themselves! A rebellion, God help us all, sir. I fear the end is near."

Durant's face closed as he pondered this information. Folly was singularly inept or luckless, but it was not likely that he would have made a mistake about this. In any case, it would be wiser to act as if he had not.

Major Folly stole a glance downward, and met the unnerving, mirthless grin of the lute player; he quickly raised his eyes and began studying the decorated ceiling intently.

"Time," Durant said. "We must have time to organize a counterattack. Major, you will . . . Major Folly! Are you listening to me?"

Folly smiled weakly and brought his gaze down to a point just above Durant's head. "I hear you, sir."

"Then look *at* me when I am speaking! And stop standing there twitching like an embarrassed schoolboy!"

It was an effort, but Folly managed it. By squinting a little, he could narrow his vision so that he could see only Lord Durant and not the youth who shared the tub with him.

"Now, Folly, you will return to Kingston and—"

"But they're on their way *here!*" Folly interrupted, The last thing he had seen behind him as he turned into the drive leading to Lord Durant's mansion was the distant shadow of a party of horsemen—miles off yet, but headed this way. There was no one it could be but minions of the aroused townspeople . . . or the pirates.

"Then stop them!"

"Stop them?" Folly repeated. He had a bitter vision of himself leaping out of the bushes in front of the approaching horsemen, raising a stern hand, and calling on them to halt in the name of the Acting Royal Governor. Seconds after he did that, Charles Austin Lepied Folly would resemble a lumpy carpet in the rough shape of a man, when the horses' hooves had done with him.

"It is your duty, Major!"

The major supposed it was, which did not help any in showing him how he was to do it. "Yes, sir," he said weakly, saluted, and retreated backward. Near the door, his scabbard inserted itself between his boots, and he made his exit in a rapid stumble. He went limp with relief when he was finally out of the room; he might be going to a futile death, but at least he was no longer in that detestable bath chamber with Durant and his eerie, abnormal companions!

Hitting every sixth step on his way, Major Folly pounded down the staircase and around a corner. He came to an abrupt halt when he found himself almost nose-to-nose with Ned Lynch, Nick Debrett, Jane Barnet, several pirates, including Mr. Moonbeam and Polonski, whom he did not recognize, and Lord Durant's secretary, whom he did—and with considerable surprise, as Culverwell was clearly not a prisoner but held a drawn sword like the others.

Ned Lynch gave a formal bow and a highly informal grin. "Major Folly . . . what a pleasant surprise."

Folly's mouth felt suddenly dry. He stared at the intruders bleakly. Lord Durant had said to stop them, and it was now or never. He wished he could have had a considerable bet down on "never." Forcing his hand to move, he reached for his sword.

"No . . . no." Ned Lynch's voice was gently reproving rather than menacing, but it froze Folly's hand to the hilt of his undrawn weapon.

"It would be a major blunder, Major Folly," Nick Debrett said kindly.

Folly gritted his teeth and said stiffly, "I have my duty, sir."

Ned Lynch corrected him. "You have your *life*, Major. The choice to keep or lose it is all yours."

"To keep it without honor is to lose it in any case," Folly said, inwardly cursing the code that made such a gesture obligatory. He whipped out his sword with a flourish. Jane remembered her own experience with standard fencing tactics against Ned Lynch, and winced. *"En garde!"* Folly cried, bracing himself for Lynch's attack.

The seven pirates and Willard Culverwell raised their swords in unison. Folly, who had expected at worst a one-sided fight against Ned Lynch, paled, then set himself in a formal fencing pose, hesitated, gulped once, and lunged at Polonski. He stopped as seven sword points formed a cone centered on his chest and only inches away from it.

Folly eyed them and the amused but implacable faces of the men who held them. Should he now rush forward once more and impale himself on the swords? Step backward and accept dishonor?

Lynch came to his aid. "Have you never heard, Major, that self-preservation is the first law of nature? Die we all must, but to die before your time, and foolishly—why, that's a *crime* against nature. Would you want your epitaph to be 'He was an *unnatural* creature'?"

In the pause that followed, Major Folly was painfully aware that the man he served could be described in no other terms than Lynch's phrase—it would be bad enough to die for Lord Durant, but to be classed with him . . .

"Thank you, Captain Lynch. As for myself"—Folly made a noble effort to regain his dignity, and at least achieved something of his customary pompousness—"I believe there comes a time in a man's life when defeat can be a greater triumph than victory."

The pirates were briefly silent, considering this unusual proposition, then Polonski politely said, "Amen," and rapped the major on the back of the head with his sword hilt; Folly collapsed bonelessly.

Debrett looked down at the handsome young officer. "If only he could be like that all the time, he wouldn't be halfbad. . . ."

The sound of an upstairs door opening—a heavy one, by the bang it made hitting the wall—came to them.

Jane tensed and looked at Ned fiercely. "Durant is mine." Lynch's eyes narrowed thoughtfully, but before he could speak, her intended victim accepted the challenge.

"Let the bitch try to take me!" Lord Durant, in tight breeches and shirt that caressed his plumpness like a second skin, stood at the landing, his sword belt buckled on. Only Willard Culverwell knew the identity of the uncanny, staring youth next to him, but all felt a chill at the sight of the steel talons projecting from his fingers.

"Villain!" Jane called.

"Whore!" Durant spat.

"Filth!"

"Catamite!"

The exchange of insults stopped as Durant, not responding to Jane's last taunt, looked down at the people in the hallway. He seemed no longer the tense, spiteful tyrant and pervert, but icily calm. "I have but one master, and his face is darkness," he murmured. It was not addressed to them, and had almost the air of a prayer.

Lord Durant slid his sword efficiently and without flourish from its scabbard and began to descend the staircase with slow, measured tread.

Jane advanced to meet him, but Ned Lynch barred her way. "No."

"Yes." She looked at him, her uncompromising stare reminding him that he had had Durant under his sword the night before—and had yielded. No matter that it had been done to save her. . . . "You *had* your chance."

Ned Lynch's face hardened. He said carefully, "Wrong, my sweet," and stepped to the foot of the stairs to meet Durant.

There was no formal salute between these two, just a heartbeat-long pause, and they began the duel.

The two rapiers circled and darted, flicked within an inch of a throat or chest before a deft parry diverted them, wove intricate figures of glittering steel in the air . . . and remained unbloodied.

In the first seconds of the fight, Jane knew that she would have died by then had she been Durant's opponent. In some ways, he was more than a match for Ned Lynch, moving with incredible lightness in spite of his layer of fat, and pressing his attack with inventive brilliance. She had the sudden horrid feeling that he was not actually doing the fighting, that some malign spirit or demon was fighting *through* him, using the Durant body and driving it to feats it should not have been capable of.

Down the hallway, through the lavishly furnished rooms, the duelists moved, circling and leaping about each other with balletlike sureness and grace; the awed onlookers followed, all sensing that this was a struggle that should not be interfered with, even if Ned Lynch fell.

A sudden rush by Durant drove Ned Lynch back, his sword beating off the other's attack, until they were once again at the foot of the staircase; the lute player had not stirred from the landing.

Lord Durant's sustained advance had told on him; overanxious for a quick victory, he had allowed himself to tire dangerously. His rapier moved less swiftly in defense, and his lunges and thrusts were less and less threatening.

The tide had turned, and Ned Lynch knew it; so did his men. And so did the taloned lute player looking down on them. He screeched once, like a strange bird, and raced down the stairs, steel-tipped hands extended, reaching for Lynch. Jane saw him first, and kicked a small chair near her; it flew into the youth's path, tripping him up near the bottom of the stairs and sending him flying through the air to the marble floor. He gave one inhuman shriek, twitched, and lay still, his right hand affixed to his chest by the steel claw on his middle finger that had pierced it.

Durant's eyes flickered toward his dead favorite for an instant—only that much for requiem and mourning, but it was too much. Ned Lynch's sword slammed on his hand, and Durant's weapon clattered to the floor.

Durant drew himself up and stared at Lynch defiantly, bracing himself for the killing thrust. Lynch eyed him, then turned and gestured to Nick Debrett, who could not understand what was wanted. All that remained was to run this baby-skinned toad through and leave this place. What could Ned want?

Lynch made it clear. "Your saber." Debrett, his practicality outraged, hestitated. Ned Lynch held out his hand. Debrett sighed and laid his sword hilt in it. Lynch hefted the saber, much heavier than his own rapier, and tossed it, hilt first, to Lord Durant.

The touch of the new weapon seemed to infuse fresh life into Durant; with tactics suited to it, he rushed Lynch, slashing, hammering, forcing him on the defensive. Skilled parrying deflected several blows harmlessly, but one wicked chop took Lynch's slender blade full on and shattered it.

Lynch's weaponless state meant nothing to Durant except a sure kill. Lynch parried one slash with his arm, taking a deep cut in his shoulder. Durant advanced, picking his spot for the final blow—would throat, head, belly be best?

"Captain!" Mr. Moonbeam's saber spun through the air, landing in Lynch's hand; he carried on the motion of its flight with a lunge that left a line of red on Durant's chest.

Face-to-face, wielding the heavy steel, taking and giving shocks that the clashing blades transmitted to wrist and arm, the two men fought savagely now, with none of the grace of the opening passage of their duel. It was to be a bloody business—and a short one, for both were tiring fast. The first to falter would lose, and

Durant's action when Lynch had been disarmed had made sure that there would be no mercy for the loser beyond that of a swift death.

Sweat poured into both their eyes, and their swings were wilder: one sweep of Durant's sword beheaded a row of candles on a table; Lynch inadvertently slashed a painting, separating two lovers portrayed in distinctly unusual union; both found themselves blundering into furniture, overturning it, and endangering themselves.

Desperation growing in him, Durant moved back toward the staircase. He cast a brief, hopeful look toward the landing, but saw no one. Yet . . .

He sprang to the stairs and retreated up them, leading Ned Lynch after him, across the landing and into his *salle d'armes;* the onlookers followed, with Jane and Nick Debrett becoming more uneasy every moment.

On familiar ground, Durant dodged among the fencing equipment and gymnastic apparatus, using them as obstacles. Twice Ned Lynch stumbled, but Durant made no effort to return to the attack; he steadily led Lynch toward a door in one wall. Reaching it, he kicked backward, opening it, and sprang through. Lynch and the others followed, and found themselves in the bathroom. The bizarre chamber startled Ned—especially the incongruous toy boats floating in the tub—and his momentary distraction gave Durant a last chance at a lunge. Lynch, stepping back from it, almost fell in the tub, then resumed his own offensive.

Durant backed past the French windows, assuring himself that they were open. Through the crack between them, he was sure he could hear the faint sound of horses' hooves and grating wheels on cobblestones. Good . . . *she* had not failed him this time—but *she* never had. . . .

Now was the time. He let his sword arm falter, clutched his chest, and held his breath. Lynch held his sword poised cautiously as the man, his face as red as that of a victim of apoplexy, seemed to gasp for breath, stare at nothing through protruding eyes, clutch at his throat, and sink writhing to the floor.

A final retching spasm convulsed him; his legs drew up and kicked, then straightened, and he was still.

Panting with exhaustion, Ned Lynch gazed down at his dead enemy. So that was the end of Durant—and past time for it. All the same, it was a letdown to have him go that way.

Jane, standing near Durant's head, felt the same way; it would have taken the sight of Durant's blood to make her feel that her and her family's wrongs had been truly righted.

With a bound, the "dead" man was on his feet, his left forearm around Jane's neck in a strangling grip, his right holding a dagger plucked from the recess of his clothing pressed into the tender flesh of her chest.

She was both shield and hostage, held between him and the pirates; the French windows were at his back. A chilling smile curved Lord Durant's full lips as he backed toward them. Jane's eyes mutely begged Ned to risk her life to take Durant's; Ned's face was expressionless. Nightmarishly, they were in the same situation as the night before.

Slowly, Durant moved toward the windows, feeling for them with one foot. He reached them, kicked them fully open, and retreated to the second-floor threshold that lay behind them. Once out there, with the pirates held at bay in the room, he would have just that single moment's start that would guarantee his escape. And there would even be time, just possibly, to slit the wench's throat once they were out of sight of Lynch and his men. . . .

Ned Lynch could read Durant's intent in his eyes. Deliberately, he lowered his saber and turned his back.

Lord Durant smiled triumphantly: once again Lynch had yielded his sword, acknowledging the force of will of a craftier and more merciless adversary. Now to step into the shadows and . . .

His eyes registered the spinning steel, though his mind could not comprehend its meaning until the saber, flung backward but with unerring accuracy over Ned Lynch's shoulder, grazed Jane's arm and sank six inches into his chest.

Lord Durant's jaw sagged. His grip on Jane's neck and on the dagger pressed to her breast did not slacken; then, terrified but exultant, she felt him sway, felt the choking arm at her throat and the pricking point of the dagger begin to falter and fall away.

Only she heard his whispered words before his hold loosened entirely. "Draw the curtain . . ." And even as he was pitching backwards into the night: ". . . The farce is played out . . ."

Close to the edge of the threshold, Jane teetered and almost fell; Ned Lynch ran to her and held her.

They looked down at the courtyard below. As if in his coffin, Durant lay where he had fallen, on the darkly lush seats of an open carriage. He stared up at them sightlessly, the saber standing straight up, as if pinning him to the rich velvet like a butterfly caught, killed, and displayed by a discriminating collector. The dark woman was in the driver's seat, sitting motionless, not giving a single glance to the corpse behind her. She flicked the reins once, and the black horses hitched to the carriage moved off at a walk, the sound of their iron-shod feet curiously muffled. The carriage rolled out of the circle of lamplight at the entryway; for a moment, before all was lost to sight in the night, the dark woman's silhouette, rising above the vehicle, could be seen.

At the end, she had not failed him.

Chapter 15

Away from the green shore, which glowed in the noon sun like a jewel on the horizon, past the squat obelisks of the Three Sisters, honeycombed with caves and tunnels, away from Jamaica and into the open sea, the *Blarney Cock* sailed. A fresh wind was in her sails; her full crew—and one or two more—were aboard and well, and there was a whole ocean to rove. If ships could feel—and hardly a man that shipped under sail wouldn't knock you down if you claimed they didn't—then the *Blarney Cock* had all that was needed to make it happy.

So, for the moment at least, did two of its inhabitants.

The fine linen coverlet on the captain's bunk heaved and billowed like a stormy sea. Presently, from beneath it came Jane's contented murmur, "Ram!"

Ned Lynch's voice was smugly lazy. "No, madam. Pirate."

On deck, the crew were at their tasks, with the usual small party at the perpetual job of painting the planking red.

Willard Culverwell, decked out in properly piratical garb from the aptly named slop chest—for which he had been told five doubloons would be deducted from his first prize shares—emerged from a hatchway and hailed Nick Debrett.

"Reporting for duty, Mr. Culverwell?"

"I am indeed, Mr. Debrett."

Nick Debrett kept himself from telling Culverwell that "I am, indeed" did not do at sea—"Aye, aye, sir" was what was wanted—but there'd be time enough for that later. "Well, listen sharply, lad: a pirate's life is not an easy one."

"Aye, Mr. Debrett." Good—he was catching on to it without even being told.

"But I would like the answer to one question."

"And what might that be?" Debrett said.

"Why do you paint the decks red?"

"Why? To cover the *blood,* lad! To cover all the blood!"

Debrett, Polonski, and Mr. Moonbeam burst into peals of laughter; Willard looked at them, wondering if that kind of carefree attitude about decks awash in blood was a necessity for a pirate, and if he could ever arrive at it . . . and if he wanted to.

Nick Debrett left the group and wandered to the rail. The laughter had left his face, and he looked soberly out to sea. The thing was done; there was no getting around it. But what would it do to Red Ned Lynch, the terror of the Indies? Could a man who set that much store by one woman be the reckless kind of pirate captain that could lead a crew to success? On the other hand, the lass was a bloodthirsty little bundle herself, and a good hand with a sword. Maybe she'd be an advantage to them. . . . He shrugged. Whichever way it was to turn out, the board had been played. Leaning his elbows on the rail, he scanned the open sea and began to hum "Johnny's Gone to Hilo."

In the captain's cabin, Ned and Jane were quiet, sated, resting. Jane smiled as Nick Debrett's humming floated down to her ears; she recalled the tune from her first stay on the ship, when, huddled and solitary on deck, she had heard Moonbeam singing it softly through the night watches. So long ago for such a few days.

She turned to Ned. "What do you think of me?"

She expected a laughing answer, but his was quiet and grave. "I think of you in ways that I have never known myself to think . . . or feel . . . or want." He fell silent, listening to his friend on the deck above. Ned joined in as Debrett reached the chorus, singing in a near-whisper:

> "Hilo, you . . .
> Hilo my Johnny's gone,
> What shall I do?
> Johnny's gone to Hilo . . ."

When the song was done, he said, "What do you think of me?"

It was Jane's turn to pause; then: "I love you."

He nodded, and they lay side-by-side listening to Nick Debrett's gentle humming, to the rush of water past the hull, to the faintly audible crack of a billowing sail, feeling the gentle motion of the ship as the *Blarney Cock* kept its true course . . . outward bound.